ONE GUY I'D NEVER DATE

A SWEET ROMANTIC COMEDY

NEVER SAY NEVER
BOOK TWO

REMI CARRINGTON

❋ Created with Vellum

ONE GUY I'D NEVER DATE

Never date your brother's best friend

There is one guy on my do-not-date list. Zach Gallagher. It's not that I'm not attracted to him. Because I've been crushing on him since I was ten.

The trouble is, he still treats me like I'm that kid who fell for him. Oh, and did I mention that he's my brother's best friend? Attraction or no, he's totally off limits.

When a Thanksgiving camping trip (which wasn't my idea) goes wrong and forces me to accept Zach's help, I have trouble remembering all the reasons he's on the list.

Then the drop-dead gorgeous deputy has the nerve to show interest, and I have to figure out how to navigate the new normal. Teasing turns into flirting . . . until my brother figures it out. He hates the idea of his little sister dating his best friend.

When Zach asks me out, I'm forced to choose, which is heart wrenching. But breaking up a twenty-year friendship is even worse. What am I going to do?

CHAPTER 1

There was one guy I'd never date. Multiple valid reasons existed for having him on a *never* list, but inconveniently, he was also the guy I compared all other guys to. Yes, it was weird. But it had nothing to do with why I was still single. Probably.

The day Zach Gallagher wandered into our yard, tossing a baseball up into the air, I fell in love. He was fourteen; I was ten.

I thought he hung the moon. But he never even looked twice in my direction. Big surprise there! I was, after all, only his friend's kid sister.

Hank and Zach were best buds. Even after high school, that didn't change. They were still friends to this day.

When I was fourteen, I'd mustered up almost enough nerve to ask Zach to the Sadie Hawkins dance—which was probably a lost cause because what senior was going to go to a dance with an eighth grader? Hank found out. That was when I learned about the rule. He waggled a finger in my face and told me sisters were never allowed to date their brother's best friend.

From that day on, Zach Gallagher was off-limits.

And Zach stayed on that *never* list way past high school—not that he was begging to be removed—because he treated me like Hank's little sister and still called me Carrot. It didn't matter that I was almost thirty.

With all that history, when Zach and his fiancée started arguing outside my apartment door, I had to eavesdrop. What choice did I have?

Lisa was my neighbor.

No, it wasn't awkward at all.

I'd never actually bumped into them together. I just spied on them when they loitered outside my door.

Not tall enough to reach the peephole, I dragged the step stool close to the door. Zach and Lisa were in the right spot. I could both see and hear.

"You care more about your friend than you do about me!" Lisa waved her arms, sobs making it hard to understand her.

She took a step toward her door but thankfully stopped. As long as they didn't move any farther to the left, I could still see. My phone rang, and Zach glanced at my door.

I answered right away . . . mostly to silence my ringtone. It was an inconvenient time to have the Mavericks singing "All You Ever do is Bring Me Down." But technically, it was a fitting song for the occasion.

I whispered a muffled, "Hello."

My best friend Eve was dating a new guy and sounded so excited.

I tried to listen and engage in the conversation with Eve while still listening to Zach and Lisa. Poor Zach looked like he needed a hug.

"Remember how I told you about Zach dating my neighbor?"

"Yeah." Eve never batted an eye when my conversation flitted from topic to topic.

I pulled away from the door to talk. The last thing I wanted was for Zach to recognize my voice. "They are standing in the breezeway outside the apartment. She doesn't look happy."

"Are you looking out your peephole?"

"So what if I am?" I kept my voice low so the couple in the hall couldn't hear me.

"I thought you couldn't stand that guy. He's the one who treats you like a kid and calls you Carrot, right? Why do you care?"

Between answers, I watched the argument through the peephole, but Eve's voice in my ear made it impossible to hear what Zach and Lisa were saying. "I don't care. It's just —never mind. I'm happy for you. To me, it seems like having Adam call you from the station is an achievement unlocked."

"It does a little. I didn't expect it."

With my attention divided between my friend on the phone and the argument in the hall, I stared through the peephole.

Zach threw his arms wide. "What did you want me to do? He . . . [muffled words] . . . rough time." I missed most of what he said because of Eve.

It probably made me a horrible friend, but I needed the call to end. "I'm going to let you go. With you talking, I can't make out what the argument is about in the hall. Bye." I ended the call before Eve could argue.

My neighbor's door slammed, and Zach was left standing in the hall, staring at the ground. For a guy so tall and lean, he suddenly looked small.

I felt a small pang of guilt for spying. But I couldn't make myself pull away. It was a good thing he didn't know I lived here. It meant I could spy with anonymity. And this scene almost deserved popcorn. But the mention of a rough time had my thoughts spinning. Was Zach referring to my brother Hank?

When my neighbor's door opened again and she tossed something at Zach, I pressed my eye closer. What had she thrown?

Zach bent down and picked up the small, shiny thing. I gasped—which ended up sounding a little like a yelp—when I realized it was a diamond ring.

His gaze shot to my door, and I backed away. Had he heard me? After a ten count, I leaned in again. He stuffed the ring in his pocket, and looking right at the peephole, he shrugged.

I felt horrible for the guy. His summer wasn't going well. Now he was also on someone else's do-not-date list.

CHAPTER 2

When my brother was dating my business partner, I thought it was great, and not only because I'd been the one to introduce them. But now that they were divorced, awkward didn't begin to describe the situation.

Thankfully, they both behaved like adults.

I packed up my camera gear before shutting down the computer. Asking about the holiday carried a risk, but I did it anyway. "Big plans for Thanksgiving?"

Nacha looked up from her computer and rubbed her eyes. "Not really. I'll pick up a holiday plate from a restaurant."

I hated that she'd be spending the holiday alone, but since I was spending it with my brother, inviting her along seemed cruel. "Have fun. I'll see you back here on Monday."

She caught my arm before I stepped away. "Could you maybe not tell him I'll be alone?"

"I won't." And it would be easy not to because Hank never asked about Nacha. Never. That was all kinds of weird.

As I drove home, I called Eve on my Bluetooth. The call

rolled to voice mail. She was probably too busy playing kissy face with her boyfriend to notice the phone—not that I blamed her. If I had a guy of my own, I'd be doing the same thing. I left a message. "Hey, it's me. Haley. Like I told you, I'm spending Thanksgiving with Hank. He asked, and I didn't feel like I could tell him no. Anyway, I'll be at his place. Tonight and tomorrow night. It's just easier to stay over there. Call me later, k?"

This was the first Thanksgiving in a long while I hadn't spent with Eve. After my parents died, her family welcomed me at every holiday meal. And her mom's blackberry swirl cheesecake was reason enough to return every year. But I couldn't in good conscience leave my brother all alone on Thanksgiving. He'd spend the whole day moping, and I'd feel guilty.

As I pulled into my parking lot, the phone rang. "Hey, Hank. I'm stopping to grab my stuff; then I'll head your way."

"Change of plans. The weather is perfect, so I booked a campsite." He wasn't laughing. "You don't mind, do you?"

"How are we going to cook a Thanksgiving meal at a campsite?" I may have raised my voice a tiny bit.

Thanksgiving required turkey, mashed potatoes, and pie. Everything else was optional.

"Same way the cavemen did it." Now he was laughing.

"Ignoring the fact that cavemen didn't celebrate Thanksgiving, I've never cooked over an open fire. I wouldn't know how to make your favorite dishes that way." I was in no way opposed to bribery as a way of getting out of camping.

"We'll all figure it out."

All? That made it sound like more people were coming. Was it too late to wiggle my way out of the invitation? "Hank, maybe I—"

"You're still going to spend Thanksgiving with your favorite brother, right?" He sounded a little hurt.

"You're my only sibling." Deadpanning was a language he understood.

Shuffling came through the line. "Then we should definitely spend time together." *It's what Mom and Dad would want.* He hadn't said that last part, but the implication was there, veiled in the humor. "Oh, and Zach is coming. Can you maybe not follow him around with that silly grin on your face?"

"I haven't done that since middle school." My gut said there would be significant regrets about agreeing to this camping trip.

"Be ready by two. I'll pick you up." He ended the call before I could argue.

Sighing more than once, I trudged to my door. Hopefully, the internet would offer guidance on what to pack.

Thirty minutes later, I was sitting on my suitcase, trying to latch it. Hank would laugh at me for overpacking, but it didn't matter what he thought.

Right at two, there was a knock at the door.

"Come in. It's unlocked." I bounced one more time, and the latch on the suitcase finally caught. "No cracks about how heavy my stuff is. You didn't give me much notice, and I wasn't sure what to take." I looked up, ready to slap down his comments.

Zach lifted his cowboy hat and smoothed his hair. "Hey there, Carrot."

"What are you doing here?" My heart used my stomach as a trampoline, then tried to come up my throat.

His eyes narrowed. He glanced at my bags then at the neighbor's door. "Let's get your stuff and go before she emerges from her den. I didn't bring any bear spray."

"Sure. Okay." Horror metastasized as I remembered him looking at the peephole. Maybe he wouldn't remember.

He picked up my suitcase and groaned. "Did you pack rocks?"

"Very funny." I locked my apartment and followed him out to his truck.

We were both buckled in before he spoke again. "You still have that stuffed dog I gave you, huh?"

Was he some kind of super spy? His focus had been on my luggage most of the time.

I was sixteen when my dog Comet died, and I'd cried for a week. It felt like my world had ended. I loved that dog. Zach had shown up with a stuffed animal that looked like a mini of Comet. He'd handed it over with hardly a word, but to me, the gesture meant the world.

I planned to keep that dog forever. It was almost always nestled into the corner of my couch. "It makes me think of Comet." That was partially true. *And you.* That was the part I didn't say.

"He was a good dog."

"The best."

Zach tapped on the steering wheel in rhythm to the music playing on the radio. "Your brother said he'd meet us out there."

"I didn't know you were camping with us. Shoot, until just a bit ago, I didn't know *I* was camping." I tried not to spit out the word camping with the distaste I felt.

"Really? Hank called me about it last month." Zach crinkled his nose. "Sorry. I probably shouldn't have told you that."

"I can't wait until Hank shows up."

We passed familiar landmarks and headed out of town.

"Don't be too hard on him. He's excited about taking you camping." He continued drumming on the steering wheel. "I'm sorry he didn't tell you. I thought he had."

"How long until we get there?"

He chuckled. "We'll get there when we get there."

"Where is Hank? Why didn't he pick me up?" Crushing on someone I'd sworn never to date was weird, and because of that, I didn't like being around Zach . . . especially alone. His green eyes and deep laugh tied my emotions in knots. And when he tousled my red curls and flashed his patronizing smile, irritation jabbed me like a pebble in my shoe.

"You're making me feel bad, Carrot. It's almost like you don't want me around."

"That's not it. It's just . . ." I couldn't exactly tell him the truth.

"Hank got a call from work, and I volunteered to babysit until he could join us."

I wanted to crawl under the seat. "Gee thanks."

His patronizing grin begged to be slapped. "You still working with Hank's ex?"

"She was my partner before he dated her, before he married her, and before she divorced him. Just because they broke up, doesn't mean my business partnership exploded." I crossed my arms, wishing I'd tempered my snark.

"Awkward, huh?" Zach ran his fingers through his short brown hair. "Sorry he put you in that position."

"Yeah."

The conversation died down after that. The rest of the drive was quiet. Time to think was not what I needed. Why hadn't my brother said something about camping? Would Eve drive out and pick me up if I asked nicely? What did Zach look like without a shirt?

Ugh! My thoughts were dangerous.

Zach showed the gate attendant a pass, then drove through the campground. We passed the restrooms, and it dawned on me that I'd have to walk there. At least I didn't have to hide behind a tree.

We passed clearing after clearing with numbers etched in wooden posts.

Finally, he turned and parked.

"What was wrong with all those spaces? The ones closer to the restrooms."

"You don't want to be by the restrooms. Besides, this is the spot we were assigned."

I hopped out of the truck, scraping together a good attitude. "What now?"

"Let's walk a bit before I unload and start dinner." Zach picked up his cowboy hat off the dash and popped it back on his head. "I'll show you the lay of the land."

"You mean there is something out here other than trees and dirt?" After his comment about babysitting, I didn't feel compelled to be nice. I didn't have enough good attitude for that. Not yet.

"Wildlife, flowers, and your favorite deputy." He patted his chest. "Grab your camera. You'll like it."

"I thought you were an investigator now." I debated about which lens to put on.

"I am. It's kind of sweet that you've kept up with my career."

"Don't flatter yourself." I opted for a telephoto lens. "I'm ready."

"Somebody didn't get a nap today." He nodded toward a trail that disappeared behind a stand of trees. "Let's head that way. I'll show you the river."

Throwing my hands into the air, I stomped. "That's enough already. I'm so sick of you and Hank treating me like I'm still ten. I'm not." I hadn't been camping even five minutes, and I'd completely embarrassed myself by acting like I was two. *Way to go, Haley!*

To make matters worse, Zach gave me a once-over. Seriously?

He quirked an eyebrow. "Clearly." Without looking back, he took off down the trail.

I followed but didn't race to keep up. The sun was still well above the trees. How hard could it be to find my way around?

Sunlight flickered through the canopy of branches. My camera clicked as I captured images of the beauty around us.

Zach stopped ahead, waiting. Showing his impatience, he tapped his foot on the ground but didn't bother to turn around. With his cowboy hat and boots, he made quite the picture . . . the perfect photo opportunity. My camera clicked again as I snagged that moment in time.

He looked back over his shoulder. "You coming?"

"I'm going to wander in here a bit. That stump is calling my name." A ray of light spotlighted a weathered stump. I shoved through a few vines and made my way closer to what was left of the old tree.

"Carrot, stop. Be careful!" Zach maneuvered his way through the trees. "You don't want to get into poison oak. It's best to stick to the trails."

"What does poison oak look like? I'll avoid it."

He pointed toward the vines I'd just pushed through. "That's poison oak."

"Crap."

Leaves rustled right behind me, and I spun around, startled by the noise. My ankle twisted, and gravity took over. Pain exploded in my side.

Fighting tears, I tried shoving myself off the ground. "Ouch!"

"You're a special kind of talented, aren't you?" Zach reached down. "Give me your hand. The one without the cactus spines in it."

Landing in a cactus only added insult to injury.

"But I managed to save my camera." I had to find a bright

spot in the situation. Between the pain and the embarrassment, my attitude wasn't adjusting in the right direction.

"And you scared a poor squirrel." Zach shook his head. "Let's get you back to camp."

I waved away his help. "I'll be okay."

"Don't be stubborn. You have cactus spines sticking out of your arm and your side." He stepped closer. "And you can barely stand up."

His statement gave me the gumption to prove him wrong. I shoved off the ground. Putting weight on my foot made my ankle scream in agony. But I bit my tongue so that I didn't do the same. "But I can walk." I was nothing if not stubborn.

"Let me at least pull the spines out."

I looked over my shoulder, trying to get a look. Resigned, I nodded.

He was much too close. "It's going to hurt."

"Do it already."

He lifted my shirt, and I jumped away, regretting the motion instantly. "What are you doing?"

"I have to pull them out of *you*, not your shirt."

I moved back toward him. "Oh."

With my shirt up, and my super pale skin exposed, Zach plucked out each spine. I set my jaw and managed not to scream. He ran his fingers over my skin, and I had to fight a different urge.

I lost the battle. Giggles exploded, and with tears flowing, I wriggled, unable to stop laughing.

Zach furrowed his brow. "Are you crying or laughing?"

I'd never seen a more confused man. "Yes. It hurts, and I'm super ticklish."

He jerked his hand away. "That's the best I can do right now. I hope that wasn't your favorite shirt."

"Why? Are there holes in it now?"

"I'm not sure the blood will wash out."

"Blood?"

"In my line of work, I've learned that people typically bleed when stabbed."

"I hadn't thought of it that way." I limped toward the trail, remembering to go around the poison oak vines. "Thanks for yanking them out."

He walked along beside me, and I think he had to walk backward every third step to keep up with me. "You realize that we're being outpaced by that snail."

"I'm sorry. This is as fast as I can move right now."

"We'll get back to camp a lot quicker if you let me carry you." He gave me the once-over again. "You'd be pretty easy to carry."

Staring down the trail, I traded my last shred of dignity for a break from the pain. "All right."

CHAPTER 3

*Z*ach set me in the truck. "Buckle up."

"What about camping?" I grabbed his arm. "Hank needs us."

"I'm never camping with you, Carrot. I live about a half hour from here. I'll tell Hank to meet us there." He slammed the truck door a little too hard.

My ankle throbbed; my side hurt; and a rash was breaking out on my arms. "I'm sorry I ruined everything."

"I'm sorry I didn't catch you."

Those words ignited an image in my head, an image I didn't need. In the last hour, I'd been closer to Zach than I had been in years. And it wasn't helping me tame my attraction. I studied him while he drove. Was he still in love with Lisa? Maybe. He still had the same smug grin that begged to be slapped away.

If I ever dared to think of removing him from the never-date list, it wouldn't matter. He wasn't at all interested. But I wouldn't take him off that list. Ever.

Thirty minutes felt like forever when everything hurt.

We neared familiar landmarks.

"I didn't know you still lived in Stadtburg." I'd grown up in this little town.

He nodded. "Saw no reason to leave."

Only a half hour from the city, it had become almost a suburb. I hadn't been back much in the three years since my parents died.

He turned off the main road into something resembling a neighborhood. But the houses were more spread out than in the city.

He parked in front of a white limestone one-story.

It was bigger than I expected—the house and the lot. The closest neighbor was half a block away.

"Don't move. I'm coming around to get you." Zach slid out and unlocked the house before opening my door. "Put your arms around my neck."

"I'll manage."

He clenched his jaw. "Do we have to have this conversation again?"

"It's not that far."

"Fine. Walk." He left the door open and headed inside. "Don't sit on my couch."

What a snot.

I eased out of the truck and yelped when my foot touched the ground. One step at a time, I hobbled to the door. All I wanted to do was sit. I made it over the threshold and stopped.

Zach had set up a folding chair.

"Thank you." I dropped into it and forced back tears.

He walked past me, drying his hands on a paper towel. "I'm getting your stuff; then you need to shower."

"Excuse me?" I'd dealt with rude people before, but this was over the top.

"Carrot, you got into poison oak. Washing off the oils is the only hope of not breaking out in a rash. It's probably too

16

late, but the hot water will help the itching anyway. It'll also prevent you from spreading the oils everywhere. After you shower, I'll doctor your wounds."

"Put the stuff where I can find it. I'm not playing doctor with you."

"Playing doctor? Seriously?" He laughed as he walked outside. "You sound like you're *ten*."

No matter what I said, he twisted it. I felt like I was back in middle school.

He walked back inside carrying my very large suitcase. "I'll put this in the bathroom. There's also a trash bag in there. Put all your clothes in it. They need to be washed." After taking my luggage down the hall, he leaned against the wall in the entryway and folded his arms. "I hope you aren't allergic to cats."

"Do you have a cat?" I glanced around, hoping to catch a glimpse of his feline.

Zach didn't exactly seem like a cat person. "No, I ask all my guests that question purely for fun." He rolled his eyes. "Yes, I have a cat."

"Where is he?"

He shrugged. "He wanders."

"What's his name?"

That wide grin made Zach's eyes twinkle. "Waldo."

I shook my head. "I walked right into that one."

"Speaking of walked. You going to walk to the bathroom?"

"Help would be nice," I mumbled.

He leaned closer. "What was that?"

"You can carry me, okay? It hurts to walk. I'm not sure how I'll even get into the tub." I couldn't even look at him. "Does that clear things up for you?"

"That's all I needed to hear." He picked me up out of the chair. "I have a plan."

17

And I was almost one hundred percent sure I wasn't going to like it.

He set me on the edge of the tub. "Get in and pull the curtain shut. Then drop your clothes over the side. I'll stay close in case you need me."

"I'm not going to shower with you in the bathroom."

"It's not like I'm going to watch you shower. I'm doing my best to be a gentleman. You need help. What if you fall in the shower? Then I'd have to call in a rescue team. Would that be better? You want your brother to show up to pull you out of the shower?"

Getting Zach's help was embarrassing, but having my brother and his work buddies show up would be horrifying.

I stuck my finger right in his face. "You can't tell anyone about this. Not a single soul."

He waved my finger away. "Especially your brother. He'd probably knock my lights out." Zach moved to the sink and faced away from the tub.

"Don't sneak any peeks in the mirror."

He covered his eyes with his hands. "Happy now?"

Sitting on the edge, I removed my socks and shoes. Taking off anything that revealed more skin would only happen behind the curtain. I pulled it closed and wriggled out of my pants, trying not to put weight on my ankle. Accomplishing the task with only a few yelps and moans felt like a victory.

One by one, my items of clothing landed on the floor. I didn't even want to think about Zach touching my bra and panties. At least I'd worn my lacy, pretty things, and they matched. "I'm turning the shower on now."

"I'll throw your clothes in the wash and be right back. Do *not* step out of that tub until I'm back."

I was in no position to argue. "Okay."

The blood on my side was a tad alarming. And the only

bottle—a shampoo, conditioner, and bodywash combo—made me smell like an Irish fisherman and stung like a hot poker being jabbed in my side. Washing, I discovered a few remaining spines. I could feel them, but I couldn't pull them out.

That meant Zach would be spending more time with his hands on my side. Mortified at the prospect, I rinsed off and waited.

How long could it possibly take to start the washer?

When I was tempted to brave getting out on my own, I pulled back the edge of the curtain.

Shirtless, Zach stood next to the sink. "You finished?"

"What happened to your shirt?"

"It's in the washer. I'm trying not to transfer oils back to you. Once I get you to the couch, I'll take a quick shower and change. For now, this is the best I can do."

The best. That word was definitely in contention for describing his chest. I hadn't seen Zach without a shirt since he shot hoops with Hank back in high school.

Zach had changed a bit . . . for the better. *Wow.* In the truck, I wondered what he looked like without a shirt, and now here he was.

"You ever going to turn off the water?"

How many ways could I embarrass myself in one night? "Don't rush me." I turned the knob, then stuck my hand around the curtain.

"Here's a towel. Cover up. I'll help you out. Then once you're out of the tub, I'll leave so you can get dressed."

I wrapped the large bath towel around me. Bless the man for having giant towels. "You don't need to pick me up. If you let me use your arm . . ."

He stuck it behind the curtain. "Please watch your step."

I gripped his arm, trying not to notice the farmer's tan or the very-toned muscles. They temporarily distracted me

19

from the pain, but only for a second. There was no way out of the tub without putting my weight on my ankle, and doing that hurt more than I could handle. "Um."

"The ankle?"

"I can't put weight on it." I didn't want to spend the rest of the night in the tub; but I also didn't want shirtless Zach picking me up when I was wearing only a towel.

"Open the curtain when you're decent."

"It's open."

He backed up toward the tub. "Put your arms around my neck. I'll give you a piggy-back ride out to the couch."

It took my brain less than half a second to dismiss that idea.

"No! Clearly, you haven't thought that one through. Absolutely not." Covered in only a towel, I was not about to wrap my legs around the man.

Every visible inch of Zach's skin turned a warm shade of pink. "I was thinking you probably didn't want me to see you in a towel, but I—never mind." He scooped me up like I weighed nothing—which was more a testament to his strength and less to my level of fitness—and carried me to the sofa. "I'll grab your bag. You can get dressed here while I take a shower. Your phone, purse, and camera bag are right there."

Getting dressed in a living room brought me to a new level of discomfort . . . until Zach walked back out with my bag.

He focused on me, his gaze sweeping over my arm and down the towel. "Will you be okay long enough for me to shower?"

I nodded. For the first time since he'd arrived at my apartment, I didn't feel like a little kid. His gaze made me feel something else entirely.

"Did I get all the spines?"

Shaking my head, I avoided his gaze. "I think there are a few still in me."

"I'll take care of those when I get back out. And I should probably take you to have that ankle checked out."

I wanted him to walk away so I could get dressed. "I sprained it. It'll be fine. Hank can look at it when he gets here."

"Promise to keep weight off that ankle?"

"I promise. Now go shower."

He strode out of the room, leaving me with a mess of emotions.

I flopped open my suitcase and stared inside. So much had happened since I'd packed, I hardly remembered what was in the suitcase. Hopefully, I'd packed pajamas that were comfortable and decent.

Flannels. Perfect.

I wriggled into my underwear, glad I brought along something not lacy. Hurrying because I wasn't sure how fast the man could shower, I slid on the pants. So far, I'd managed to keep the towel around me, but getting the shirt on would be easier without the towel. With all my cactus wounds, a bra was out of the question, but thankfully, my pajama shirt was baggy.

I let the towel fall and slipped my arms into the sleeves, then rushed to button up the front. But with my talent for messing things up, I'd put the shirt on inside out.

Tugging the shirt off, I prayed he wouldn't come darting out.

The sleeves had gotten pulled inside out. Getting my arm through wasn't going to happen unless I fixed it.

I strained to hear the water in the pipes. Had it stopped running?

With the sleeves the way they needed to be, I put the shirt on the right way and rushed to button it up.

Hurried and flustered, I started at the top button and worked my way down.

As I buttoned that last one, my phone rang. Eve was calling.

I really needed to change my ringtone. Pasting on a smile, I prepared to fake my way through the conversation.

"How are you? I got your message earlier, but I couldn't sneak away to call until now." Eve sounded bubbly.

"Things are good. I mean, it isn't what I expected . . . at all."

"Did Hank invite Zach along?"

What part of my tone gave any hint that Zach was here? Lying to my best friend was a pointless endeavor, but I wasn't ready to give up trying. "Yeah, but it's not a big deal."

"Tell Zach I said sorry about his breakup."

I gasped. "I am not bringing that up. Then he'll know."

We'd somehow managed to make it this far through the evening without bringing up the whole spying through the peephole episode. He'd probably forgotten about it, and I didn't want to remind him.

"Then I'll know what, Carrot?" Zach walked up, his hair still dripping wet.

Eve laughed. "I'll talk to you later. Text me if you live through the night."

"Very funny." I wasn't amused because she didn't know the half of it. Dying was a real threat. I glanced up, prepared to ignore his question. "Did you even dry off?"

"I just took the fastest shower ever so I could get back out here to help you." He held up his arms. "But I didn't get the oil off in time."

Guilt was an unwelcome companion. "I'm sorry." Tears stung my eyes, and I blinked, hoping he wouldn't notice.

"Whatever you do, don't cry. I had about all I can take of that in the park."

Why did every word out of his mouth get my dander up?

"Let me grab the tweezers." He continued toweling off his hair as he walked out of the room.

When he walked back to the couch, I stretched out and rolled onto my good side. "Did you lock the door? We don't want Hank walking in unexpectedly." I didn't need my brother misinterpreting the situation.

"He texted to tell me he's working all night." Zach handed me a pillow, then pulled a chair close to the couch. "Let me see your arm. Is that ticklish?"

"Not as much." Every inch of me was ticklish to varying degrees.

For the next seven minutes, he plucked spines out of my arm. "I can't believe I missed so many." His rough, warm fingers trailed over my skin. "All right, I covered that area in antibiotic cream. Now for the ticklish part."

I lifted my shirt and held my breath. I could do this. But as soon as he touched me, giggles erupted again. I buried my face in the pillow. "Just do what you have to."

"Slap me if I hurt you."

"I may do that anyway." Tensing and giggling, I let the pillow catch my tears. Yanking out the little spines hurt as much as pulling out the big ones.

When he finished, he tugged my shirt back into place. "Now to deal with your ankle."

"It's fine." I shifted back into a sitting position.

He knelt on the floor and picked up my foot. "Your ankle is not fine. It's swollen and bruised. I need to wrap it; then we'll get ice on it." Shockingly, his fingers didn't leave scorch marks as they grazed over my skin.

Carefully, he wrapped an elastic bandage around my foot. "Let me know if it's too tight. I don't want your toes turning purple." After crisscrossing it over my foot, he finished

23

winding it around my lower leg and fixed it in place with the Velcro end. "How's that? Can you move it?"

I tried rotating my ankle. "Not really."

His rough fingers brushed my toes. "Any tingling here?"

Now there was, but it was only because the man kept touching me. It had nothing to do with the bandage on my ankle. "I don't think it's cutting off circulation."

"Good. Let me grab you ice." He left the room and returned with an ice pack and a couple of pillows. "Put your ankle up and wrap this cold pack around it."

"You like to give orders, don't you?" Cranky best described my current mood.

He leaned over me. "Haley, if it isn't too much trouble could you—pretty please—elevate your ankle and ice it so that the swelling will go down and the pain will ease?"

"I liked it better when you gave orders."

"I'll remember that." He winked. "I'm going to make dinner. Holler if you need anything. And by that I mean, don't move until I come back."

I stuck my tongue out at his back as he walked away. So much for not acting like I was ten.

CHAPTER 4

"*Y*ou want to eat in here or on the patio? I can get a fire going out there." Zach gazed out the back door. "It's a nice evening." It wasn't hard to tell what he wanted.

After going all day without food, I was ready to eat anywhere. "Outside is fine."

"Let me get the firepit going; then I'll come get you. I made chili."

"Did you put beans in it?" I was a tad picky about my food.

"I was going to." He rolled his eyes. "But I won't."

"Thanks."

Shaking his head, he walked out the back door.

I poked at the pink patches on my arms. The anti-itch medicine helped a little, but between the pain and itching, I wasn't sure how I'd be able to sleep tonight.

While Zach banged around in the kitchen and carried stuff outside, I sat helpless.

A few minutes later, he walked up. "You know the drill."

I looped my arms around his neck, and he lifted me off the couch.

Stopping next to a lounge chair, he looked down at me. "Are we going to talk about what I'll know that you don't want me to know? Or perhaps I already know it but haven't said anything. Did you think of that?"

My body tensed. Even the threat of death wouldn't make me want to tell Zach that I'd spied on his breakup. There was no way he could know, right?

Laugh lines appeared near his eyes. "Seems like you aren't ready for that conversation. We can save it for later. What did your friend say about all this?" Firelight reflected in his green eyes.

It could've been arctic temperatures outside, and I wouldn't have noticed. "I thought we agreed we wouldn't tell a soul."

"Good." He winked. "You passed the test." Gently, he nestled me into the chair. "I'll grab you a blanket and bring you a bowl of chili. Want cheese on it?"

Are you as hot as pavement on an August day in Texas? "Sure. That'd be great."

Lounge chairs circled a firepit that was surrounded by a limestone wall. Off to the right, there was a full outdoor kitchen with a grill and sink. To the left, was a large patio table and eight chairs.

Zach dropped a blanket near my feet and handed me a bowl.

"Your house is nice, but this patio is incredible."

"I come out here and have coffee in the morning most days, and the view from here as the sun creeps up into the sky is amazing." His spoon clinked against the side of his bowl. "I'm happy I found this house."

I pulled the blanket up, then started in on the chili. "So good. Thank you. I haven't had anything but coffee all day."

"You shouldn't do that. It's not good for you." Even trying to be nice, he could be seriously annoying.

"How 'bout we skip the telling-me-what-to-do part."

He chuckled.

The sound of the crackling fire relaxed me as I filled my tummy.

"How's the photography business?"

I stopped eating long enough to answer. "It's going really well. I'm lucky to get paid for doing what I love."

"You sure paid for it today." He set his bowl aside and leaned back in his chair.

"Very funny. I don't know why y'all enjoy camping so much. It wasn't all that fun." I finished my last bite.

"We stay away from the poison oak and cactus. You managed to find every dangerous thing except a rattlesnake, and it's too cold for them right now." He picked up the bowls. "More?"

"No. It was good though." I caught his arm as he stepped away. "Will you bring me my camera?"

"Yep." Moments later, he set the camera bag in my lap, then walked off into the shadows.

By the time he returned, my camera was ready. When he tossed logs on the fire, I pushed down on the shutter and captured a series of pictures of the sparks dancing in the air. And as he poked at the fire, shoving the logs into place, I took pictures of his hands.

He dropped back into his chair and pulled a bag and a cooler closer to him. "Get anything good?"

"I think so. I'll know better when I see it on a bigger screen."

"Moon pie?" Zach held one out to me.

"Where did you find this? I haven't had these in ages." Once upon a time, Moon Pies were my favorite dessert. "All I need now is an RC Cola."

He leaned back and pulled one out of the cooler. "Here you go."

"Do you live your life prepared to act out lines of a country song?" I pinched off a bite, reminding myself to eat slowly.

"You have me all figured out." He pulled another two Moon Pies out of his bag of goodies. "There's another one here when you finish."

"Thanks." Starting out rotten, the evening had turned around. Completely. Granted, my arms itched; I had bandages and ointment on my side; and my ankle was twice its size, but getting this chance to hang out with Zach was totally worth it.

"What aren't you going to bring up?" He had to go and ruin the night.

"What part of not bringing it up confuses you?" I popped the last bite in my mouth, then reached for the other Moon Pie.

One side of his mouth lifted in a grin. "All right then. If I bring it up, then can we talk about it?"

"Sure." I felt safe letting him have his fun. After tearing away the plastic wrapper, I bit into my second helping of dessert. "Don't pull out any more of these. I don't care how many you have stashed in that bag."

"Yes, ma'am." He wandered inside, then reappeared with a guitar. For a few minutes, he strummed, and music danced in the breeze. "I'm a little surprised you haven't mentioned my failed engagement."

I gasped, and a small chunk of cookie lodged in my windpipe. Trying to get air into my lungs, my mouth gaped open. I'm sure it was a great look.

Zach still had his gaze fixed on the fire.

Panicked, I kicked his chair and waved my arms.

He raised his head, and in a second, he had his arms around me, doing the Heimlich.

My piece of Moon Pie went flying and landed in the firepit. I inhaled a welcome lungful of air. "Thank you." Chest heaving, I relaxed into his arms.

He pulled away like I was on fire. "It was because of your gasp."

"Thank you, Einstein. Yes, I know why I choked." I tossed the last little bit of Moon Pie into the fire. They were as dangerous as camping.

He sat on the edge of his chair and leaned toward me. "You okay?"

I nodded and washed down the bitter taste of embarrassment with my RC Cola.

He dragged his fingers through his hair. "I meant that I knew you saw the argument because of your gasp. Every time Hank and I did anything remotely dangerous—"

"Which was all the time." Now that my heart wasn't beating like a drum solo at a rock concert, I realized how much pain accompanied every breath.

He rested his elbows on his knees. "Anyway, I've heard that gasp enough times to recognize it. Besides, I knew you lived there, and I recognized your ringtone. Well-timed by the way. It was true. She knew how to bring me down. Be right back." He ran inside and returned with a bottle of over-the-counter pain pills. "You'll probably need those. I might've bruised a rib. And I'm sorry about that."

I reached for the bottle, trying not to touch his fingers in the exchange. "I'm sorry about your breakup."

"I was too *for a while*." With a small stick, he scratched at the rock wall around the firepit. "But it's for the best. We weren't good for each other."

"Still. The way she did it was a tad heartless."

"Just a bit." He dropped the stick and went back to playing the guitar.

For several minutes, the crickets and cicadas harmonized with his music, and I contemplated how it might feel to trail my fingers through the short hairs at the nape of his neck. In any other scenario, I'd love sharing a moment like this with a gorgeous hunk of a man while he played the guitar. Romantic was the word to describe it. Except, this was Zach. And with Zach, I was not supposed to feel this way. There were rules.

After setting the guitar aside, he stood and dusted off his backside. Intentionally not watching his hands, I stared at the fire.

"You ready for bed? It's been one heck of a day."

"Yeah." I dutifully wrapped my arms around his neck when he leaned down. "Thanks for everything today. And especially for not letting me die a bit ago."

"I'm sorry I hurt you, but I would've broken a rib if that was required to keep you alive. In my line of work, if I showed up and found a dead woman on the back porch and she was in the shape you're in, I'd haul the guy in for battery and possibly murder. I didn't want that to be me."

"How considerate of you." I grinned as he sat me down, hoping it hid my wince. "Good night."

He nodded as he walked away. What did he have against saying good night? The lights switched off one by one. In the dark, the house had a different feel.

When a black shadow approached, I took a guess that it was Zach. "Did you forget something?"

"Nope. Just rolling out my sleeping bag."

I reached out and grabbed his arm. "No . . . you can't sleep on the floor." *Next to me.*

"Considering you can't walk and can barely breathe without pain, I figured you might need someone close. And sleeping on the living room floor seemed a better alternative than suggesting we go into one of the bedrooms."

"You're right. Thank you." What else could I say?

In the dark, neither of us moved for a full second.

"Carrot."

My stomach felt like someone had pumped it full of pop rocks and poured soda on top. "Yes?"

"You ever going to let go of my arm?" Even in the dark, his patronizing grin was obvious. The words sounded different whenever he smiled that way.

I yanked my hand back. So much for not embarrassing myself. Again.

CHAPTER 5

*W*as it possible for a bladder to burst? I was going to find out if I lay here any longer.

On the floor, Zach was sprawled on his stomach, his arms crossed under his head. And he was snoring, which meant he wouldn't snap at me about staying put. I'd already overdosed on embarrassment.

I sat up and untangled myself from the covers. Clenching my jaw and gripping the couch, I rose, putting weight on my ankle. Then I dropped back onto the sofa. That wasn't going to work.

My full bladder didn't allow for clear thinking or brilliant ideas. I'd have to endure the pain.

About to shove myself up, I stopped when his snoring silenced. He turned his head toward the couch. Were his eyes still closed?

"Stay put. What do you need? I'll get it." He blinked, as if trying to force his eyes open.

"Unless you've figured out some magical way to go to the bathroom for me, that won't work." I leaned forward, determined not to scream when I stood.

"I'll carry you." He scrubbed his face.

"No. Go to sleep. I'll figure it out." I was tired of being carried, which surprised even me. After a few steps, I dropped to the floor and crawled the rest of the way to the bathroom. The method wasn't pretty, but it was functional.

When I crawled back out, Zach sat beside the sofa, shaking his head. "It would've been easier and faster if I'd carried you." He held out his hand when I stopped in front of the sofa.

"You've done enough of that." Using his hand, I maneuvered my way back onto the cushions. "But thank you for being sweet."

He nodded and stood. "I need a snack. Want anything?"

"What kind of snack?"

"Why don't I make us a batch of my snackalicious popcorn?" He padded off to the kitchen in his bare feet.

Pans clinked and rattled, and I waited. Snacking at two in the morning was crazy. The whole day had been nuts. I'd never spent so much time alone with Zach, and seeing this other side of him wasn't doing great things for my resolve to keep him on the *never* list.

Carrying a large bowl, he nodded for me to scooch over, then dropped down beside me. "This is a secret recipe. It cannot be shared. Promise?"

I crossed my heart.

"My favorite late-night snack. It's a mix of popcorn, M&M's, mini marshmallows, caramel bits—the kind from the baking aisle—white chocolate chips, and cashews. It's important that you get popcorn that doesn't just half pop and leave lots of kernels. Then it's no fun to eat." He scooped some into a cup and handed it to me. "Enjoy."

"Do you always have this stuff in your pantry?"

"I keep this stuff in my pantry so I can make this *delicious snack* whenever I want." A handful disappeared into his mouth, and he grinned. "You ever going to try it? Oh, the good stuff sinks to the bottom. That's why I use a cup."

Instead of picking at it one piece at a time, I followed his lead and grabbed a handful. I fell in love. Again. "Oh my gosh. How have I lived until now without this? It's amazing."

"Told you." He tossed an M&M in the air and then caught it in his mouth. "How's your pain? Need more meds?"

"Probably not a bad idea."

"If the pain in your chest doesn't start to ease, we'll need to get you x-rayed. I'm hoping I didn't crack a rib."

I launched a puff of popcorn into the air and tried to catch it.

Zach howled with laughter when it flew down my pajama shirt. "I wonder if I could do that." He tossed a marshmallow at me.

"Behave." I shook the bottom of my shirt until the popcorn fell out. "And I think my ribs are okay. But laughing isn't helping, so stop being funny."

He tousled my curls. "You're too funny. Mind if I turn something on?"

"That's fine. I'm not sleeping until this bowl is empty anyway." I refilled my cup.

After a few clicks of the remote, a show started. "Mandalorian. I haven't seen the latest episode. Have you been watching it?"

"Never heard of it." Based on the intro playing out on the screen, it had something to do with Star Wars.

"Then we'll start with episode one." He clicked play.

With him at one end of the sofa and me at the other, we watched the show.

The popcorn lasted through one and a half episodes.

When the second episode ended, I was willing to watch another, but Zach yawned.

"We'll watch more tomorrow. I'm tired." He picked up the

empty bowl. "I can't believe your brother hasn't introduced you to that show."

I snuggled back under the blanket. "We didn't exactly spend a lot of time together until he moved back to town after the Montana thing."

"He hasn't been the same since the divorce."

"You're right. He's been different. Now he wants to get together for dinner, spend holidays together, and stuff like that. I don't mind, but I'm worried about him."

"We'll have to be intentional about keeping him busy." Zach switched off the lights.

In the dark, I rolled onto my side and watched him settle back into place. "Zach."

"Yes?"

I felt like an eighth grader all over again. "This was fun."

"It was. And it's probably best not to talk about this part to your brother. Night, Carrot."

"Good night."

Did saying we shouldn't tell my brother imply anything about what tonight meant to Zach? Was his heart fluttering like mine?

* * *

USUALLY I WAS UP EARLY ENOUGH to greet the sun. But after the day I'd had and the middle-of-the-night snacking, I slept in.

Voices in the kitchen woke me.

"I'm not sure how I feel about you having my sister spend the night. I know you're lonely after your fiancée dumped you, but this is sinking pretty low."

"Stop it, Hank. Nothing happened. It's Haley. She's practically—" Zach didn't finish his sentence, but I knew what was going to fill in the blank.

"Practically what?" Hank was almost shouting.

"She's just Carrot, okay?"

Just Carrot.

All my warm fuzzies turned to ice. I stood, and gritting my teeth, I hobbled to the bathroom. Zach could keep Hank company for Thanksgiving. I wanted to go home.

Getting dressed was a small chore, but I managed. With the suitcase dangling from my uninjured hand, I opened the bathroom door.

Zach blocked my exit. "You're up."

"Yep. I think I'm going to head on home. But I'll call for a ride."

He glanced over his shoulder and rested his hands on the doorframe. "You don't need to run away. He knows nothing happened."

"Why would anyone think something happened? Everyone knows sisters never date their brother's friends." I ducked under his arm but stopped when I felt a tug on my hair. "What?"

"Stay."

"Why? If I leave, the two of you can go back out to your campsite and fish until you catch your dinner." I didn't know how to act like his words didn't hurt.

Zach pinched his lips together. "Because your brother is excited about spending Thanksgiving with his family. That's you and me, Carrot. *Both of us.*"

I limped down the hall. "I'll see how the day goes." The front door closed, and I turned to face Zach. "Hank's leaving?"

"Left to pick up the food. He ordered sides. We're cooking the turkey." Zach looked down at my ankle. "It's swelling again."

"So that's what he had planned all along." I kept a hand on the wall and hopped a few steps.

"We didn't expect you to cook for us." Zach positioned himself at the end of the wall and put his arm out. "I'll get you ice, and you can elevate it."

I set the suitcase down. Clutching his arm, I leaned into him more than was appropriate after hearing what he'd said to Hank. "I think I'd like to sit out on the patio."

Zach nodded.

"Thanks for setting things straight with Hank."

"For someone who had no problem letting me spend the night in a tent with you, he sure got weird about you being here."

I laughed, then winced.

"Sorry about that. Ribs still hurt?"

"A little. Can we stop for a second?" Hopping jostled every muscle, and my whole body was sore for one reason or another. I felt like the coyote after he'd failed to catch the roadrunner a hundred times or more.

"We probably need to find you some crutches."

"I have some at my apartment. This isn't my first sprain." I patted his arm. "All right. I'm ready."

"For me to carry you?" He glanced at the door. "Using this method, we'll still be all cozy when your brother gets back, and that might be a bad idea."

"You have a valid point."

"And the longer you are upright, the more that ankle swells." He raised his eyebrows, waiting for permission.

I squeezed his arm, as much for sheer enjoyment as to give him his answer. "You going to pick me up, or should I jump?"

CHAPTER 6

*W*ith camera in hand, I passed the time taking pictures. "Is that your cat?"

"Where?"

I pointed at a tail, visible on the other side of a feed trough set up as a planter. "The orange striped fuzzy one."

"Yeah, that's him." Zach opened the cooler. "Want anything?"

"If there's another RC Cola in there, I'll be a happy camper."

"Very funny, considering." He popped the top off the bottle and handed it over.

"How long have you had the cat? And where did you get it? You don't seem like a cat person."

"I'll have you know I love cats . . . and dogs. I'm an animal person."

"Even snakes?" Just the thought of the slithery creatures bothered me.

"I'm not a fan of the ones that can kill me. But I've owned a few rat snakes." He drank down a swallow of Big Red. "And

Waldo's been around about two years. I arrested him not long after I moved into this place."

"You arrested him?"

Zach grinned and dropped into a chair. "We were investigating a theft. A woman had called in, worried because her *pretty things* had been stolen off the clothesline and out of her laundry basket. She was worried she had a stalker or something."

I wasn't about to let Zach off easy. "Pretty things?"

"Lacy. Like yours, which I need to get out of the dryer for you." Hopefully, he hadn't used a high heat setting, or nothing would fit the same way ever again.

"Yes, but please continue."

"Anyway, we were in her kitchen, finishing up the report, and a cat grabbed one of her bras and dragged it off. I started laughing, which wasn't a great idea. But she forgave me when she turned around." Zach crossed his arms over his chest. "We asked around to see if the cat had an owner, but he didn't. Poor guy was a stray, so I brought him home. So, if you ever find any pretties lying around, blame Waldo . . . not me."

"He still steals things?"

"I haven't found a stash, but he probably wouldn't tell me if he did."

"I'm back," Hank hollered as he walked through the house. "You can start the turkey, and I'll warm these sides."

Zach jumped up. "I made mashed potatoes to go with everything."

"Is that why you were banging around in the kitchen?" Knowing mashed potatoes were on the menu made me feel a little bit better.

"Yep. Making whipped mashed potatoes like my grandma used to." He ran inside, leaving me to take more pictures.

In the last twenty-four hours, I'd talked to Zach more

than I had in all of middle school and high school. He was so much more attractive now . . . inside and out. Those kinds of thoughts did not help me.

Just Carrot. That reminder would have to get me through today.

The guys lowered the turkey into the bubbling oil, and I got hungrier by the second.

Even the fast method wasn't instant.

When they lifted the turkey out of the oil forty-five minutes later, Zach winked. "Looks gooooood. Now it has to sit a few minutes."

"My patience is running out." I took off the telephoto lens and tucked the camera and accessories back into place.

Hank laughed. "You never had any to begin with."

The guys disappeared inside, and I inched to the edge of the chair. I plotted my route, looking for things to hold on to while I hopped to the table.

I pushed off the chair, and Zach peeked his head out the door.

"Sit."

"I'm more than a little tired of you acting like a dictator." Balancing on one foot wasn't all that easy with sore ribs.

He strolled up and planted himself in front of me. "I wouldn't have to if you'd listen to me."

"You're infuriating." I wobbled but refused to drop back into the chair. Clinging to the back of it, I fought to keep my balance.

He stuck his hand out. "And you're—"

"Are y'all coming or not?" Hank was the one who was impatient.

I grabbed Zach's hand to keep from falling over.

He swallowed. "Come on, Hop-a-long, let's get you to the table."

"You didn't finish your sentence." I searched his face for any hint to what he was about to say.

He smiled down at me. "You can wonder about it."

The man was infuriating and maddening. Coming from anyone else, I would take that as flirting, but this was Zach, and I was just Carrot.

I settled at the table, almost as excited about the whipped mashed potatoes as I was about the turkey. The guys carried the foil pans to the table; then Zach set a pot right in front of me.

To my horror, there were peas mixed in. "Who puts peas in their mashed potatoes?"

"My grandma. Why?" Zach carved the turkey.

"You ruined a perfectly good dish."

Zach laughed. "No beans. No peas. Does Carrot not like her vegetables? Although, beans are legumes, not vegetables. You like carrots, though, right? I mean, it wouldn't seem right if you didn't."

"Leave me alone." I served myself a spoonful of what he'd made, planning to eat around the peas.

"She hates anything green. And a few things that aren't green. Mostly just healthy stuff." Hank pushed the pan of green bean casserole closer. "Want any?"

Teasing from my brother wasn't nearly as tolerable as it was from Zach.

"I'll take dark meat." I held out my plate.

Zach served me juicy slices of turkey.

How had I ended up sitting across from him? And why was it that every time I glanced up, he made eye contact? When our eyes met, butterflies danced the cha-cha in my belly.

"When is your next photo shoot?" Hank pointed at my foot then served himself seconds.

I finished chewing my bite of food. "I have a Hill Country shoot late next week."

"Need help?" He was a good big brother, but having him around would be a disaster.

I shook my head. "I'll be fine. Nacha will be there."

"Good. You won't be out there alone." He focused on his plate. "I'm working anyway."

"Will you be able to keep weight off it while you take pictures?" Zach pulled the potatoes and peas closer to his plate.

"Oh yeah. But I should probably go home after dinner to dig out my crutches and maybe practice a little."

"I'll run you home." Hank leaned back in his chair. "But not before we have dessert."

Guilt rattled around in my head when I wished Hank would get called back into work or discover he was out of gas . . . any reason that would change things so that Zach would have to take me home.

"Practice? That sounds dangerous." Zach cleared plates off the table. "Do we want dessert now or later?"

"Now." Hank always wanted dessert. We were clearly related. He jumped up and headed toward the kitchen. "I'll bring the pies to the table."

Zach followed Hank into the kitchen.

A few minutes later, Zach leaned over the back of my chair. "Your bag was open a little, so I put your things on top."

Before I could say anything, Hank rounded the corner, and Zach moved to his chair like he'd developed the super-power of speed.

Maybe it was best that Zach wasn't driving me home. Being around him was chipping away at my sanity.

CHAPTER 7

*E*ve tossed a treat to her cat, then dropped onto the sofa. "You've hardly said anything about how yesterday went. I'm dying to know. You haven't even told me how you ended up with a sprain."

I was dying to talk about it, but only certain parts, and I needed to give some explanation of my wounds. "Hank ended up having to work Wednesday night, and I spent the night with Zach."

My friend almost fell off the couch. "You what?"

"That came out wrong. He picked me up—from my apartment, I mean." I didn't want to talk about how he'd carried me around. "We'd been at the campsite only a few minutes when I walked through poison oak"—I held up my arms to show off the rash—"then twisted my ankle and fell into cactus."

She slapped a hand over her mouth. "No way."

I lifted my shirt to show off the little red marks from the spines. "Anyway, we didn't end up camping. I ended up staying the night on his couch."

Eve laughed. "Oh my! It's like a dream come true and a nightmare all at once."

"Until he told my brother I was *just Carrot,* then it was all nightmare." I sighed.

"Would you go out with him?"

Rubbing my ankle, I delayed my answer. "Going out involves two people being interested. So, no. Besides, Hank was weird about it when he showed up at the house. Pretty sure he wouldn't approve."

"How many times has your brother asked you about the ladies he dates?"

"I get your point, but Zach is Hank's best friend. There are rules and expectations for this type of thing. Besides, getting back to my original point, I'm still just Hank's kid sister." I shoveled ice cream into my mouth. "I learned that Zach has a cat that steals ladies' underwear."

Eve giggled. "That could be embarrassing."

"Tell me about it."

Waldo was probably to blame for my missing underwear. That was the only item missing from the top of my bag. Either Waldo had returned to a life of crime, or—I couldn't even contemplate the other option. But Eve didn't need to know any of that.

"Want me to see if Adam has a friend? A blind date worked for me." She added extra gummy bears to her vanilla ice cream.

"I'll think about it." Getting over my crush on Zach required me to get out of my comfort zone.

She waved her spoon back and forth. "I want you to be happy. You know that, right?"

"I know." I set my empty bowl aside. "I'll give you an answer by the end of the weekend."

"Harper. I'll ask Adam about his friend Harper, but I'll wait until you decide."

Dating a firefighter sounded exciting . . . almost as exciting as dating a law enforcement officer.

That type of thinking would keep me stuck. I needed to move on.

* * *

THANKFUL that my camera bag could be worn crossbody, I hobbled toward the barn. "Nacha, thanks for driving."

Nacha slowed her pace so that I could keep up. "I wasn't going to let you drive. That ankle looks terrible."

"It's been more than a week. I was hoping it would be better by now." Getting the hang of the crutches hadn't taken as long as I thought it would. "What if we set up the boots on that rock and get the weathered red of the barn in the background?"

"That would work." Nacha positioned the rhinestone-studded boots at the perfect angle. The light rays made the pair sparkle. "Wasn't our model supposed to meet us out here?"

"Yep. I texted her the location." I sat on an old stump and dropped my crutches. The camera was ready in no time flat, and I pressed the shutter a few times before studying the images in the viewfinder.

Nacha stepped away when her phone buzzed, leaving me to take more pictures.

Choosing my steps carefully—because walking barefoot out here carried the risk of being bitten, punctured, or pricked—I hobbled over to the boots, breaking my promise to Zach, but he wasn't here to scold me. After shifting the pair so that there was a field of green and blue sky as a backdrop, I limped back to my stump.

"That was Cami. She had a flat not far from here. I'm

going to run and get her. Will you be okay for a few minutes?"

"I'll be fine. I want to get this wrapped up so I can make it back home in time for my date." The idea of a blind date still made me nervous.

"Don't hurt yourself. I'll be back as soon as I can." She climbed back into the car and bumped along the dirt path toward the gate.

I tried to envision other ways to stage the boots. Using a shallow depth of field, a picture with the boots perched on the stump would be eye-catching. I picked up my bag and crutches and moved them out of the shot. Once the boots were sitting in place, I dropped to the ground. My ankle throbbed because I didn't have the sense to keep weight off it.

With the boots framed perfectly and the evening light adding a warm glow, I focused my camera. As I mashed the shutter, a silver pickup pulled into the gate.

Who had messed up my shot? I shaded my eyes against the setting sun, trying to make out the driver.

Suddenly, I felt very alone in that field. My only hope of defense was ninja skills with my crutches. Truth be told, my ninja skills were lacking.

Alternating glances between the ground and the truck, I scooted toward the barn. Getting up without something to grab onto wasn't going to happen.

The truck stopped, and when the driver stepped out, my heart stopped too.

Why was Zach here? As I took in his jeans and western dress shirt, I tried to maintain even breaths.

He grinned as he set his hat atop is head. "Hey there."

"Why are you here? And that isn't your Explorer." I didn't even bother trying to stand up.

"That's my work truck." Zach looked down at me. "I'm

responding to a trespassing call. Someone nearby called in about a redhead on crutches taking pictures near the abandoned barn."

"We have permission from the landowner to be here."

He held out his hand. "Did you walk here alone?"

"Nacha had to go pick up the woman who is going to model the boots. Her car broke down." I grabbed his hand and let him pull me to my feet.

"It's still swollen."

I nodded. "I was hoping to wear my boots tonight on my date, but that's clearly not happening."

"On your what?" Zach furrowed his brow. Why was he making it awkward?

I rubbed my forehead. "A date."

"Has Hank met the guy?" He rested a hand on the barn wall behind me and leaned closer.

"I haven't even met him. It's a *blind date*."

Where was Nacha?

"Do you trust the person who set you up? Where is he taking you?"

"He's a fireman, a good friend of my best friend's boyfriend. And I don't know where we're going."

"So basically, he's a friend of a friend of a friend. Where are you meeting him?"

I pressed a hand to Zach's chest. "Back up. What's with all the questions?"

"I'm looking out for you." He blinked and stepped back. "Sorry. Didn't mean to crowd you."

"While I appreciate the thought, you don't need to do that." My hand had been on his chest way too long, so I yanked it back.

"Duly scolded. Didn't mean to treat you like you were ten." He winked.

The Mavericks started singing "All you ever do is bring

me down," and he looked at my phone lying on the ground. "Would you like me to get that?"

"Yes, please."

He handed it over, then walked back to the truck.

"Hello?"

Nacha sighed. "There won't be a photo shoot today. Someone hit Cami's car while it was on the shoulder. As soon as the police are finished, I'll run back and get you. I'm so sorry."

Zach stood beside his truck, watching me.

"Don't worry about it." I motioned him back toward the barn. "I might be able to get a ride. I'll text you. Bye."

"Did Nacha abandon you?" Zach's humor was anything but subtle.

I propped a fist on my hip. "Nacha didn't abandon *anyone*."

"It was a joke." He shielded himself with his hands. "But clearly not a funny one."

"If it isn't funny, it doesn't qualify as a joke."

"Good point. So what's up?" He kept his distance.

Spending time with Zach right before my blind date was a bad idea. I knew that. "She's stuck while the lady fills out a police report. Someone hit her car on the shoulder. And—"

"You need a ride so you can be home in time for your date, right?"

"That's what I was going to ask you."

He nodded. "Tell me what to gather. You need to keep weight off that ankle so it doesn't throb all evening."

"Will you help me to the stump?"

"Sure."

When he leaned in close, I snaked my arms around his neck. "It'll be faster if I let you carry me."

Without a word, he scooped me up. Why did being in Zach's arms have to feel so good?

Harper couldn't compete with this . . . unless of course, he was actually interested.

After putting me down, Zach held up a finger. "Make me one promise."

"I'm doing my best to keep weight off it."

"Not that." He pinched his lips together. "Don't let him carry you."

"I don't foresee that happening, Zach. You're the only one crazy enough to tote me around."

He tugged at the end of a curl. "Promise me."

I crossed my heart. "I won't let him."

CHAPTER 8

I smoothed my dress, giving myself a pep talk. "Forget Zach. You're going out with Harper. You want to have a nice evening . . . crutches and all." Snatching up the phone, I hurriedly called Eve.

"You aren't cancelling, are you?"

"Did you tell Harper I was on crutches?" Deep breaths weren't helping me stay calm.

"Yes. He knows." She laughed. "No excuses. He'll be there any second."

A knock sounded right on time.

"I think he's here. Bye." I inhaled once more, hoping this deep breath would do the trick. When I opened the door, I froze. "Hi."

The man at the door had green eyes. Why couldn't they be brown or blue or pink?

He stuck his hand out. "I'm Ethan, but you probably know me as Harper. That's what most people call me."

"Nice to meet you. I'm Haley. And most people call me Haley." Way to sound smart right off the bat. "Let me grab my crutches, and I'll be ready."

"What did you do to your ankle?"

"Turned it when I went camping." That sounded better than I heard a noise and turned around.

"Well, it's a good thing you live on the ground level. But if you need me to, I can carry you. We get training for that in firefighter school."

I stopped my hobble. "I don't need you to carry me."

Harper laughed. "That was supposed to be funny. I mean, I did get training for that, but considering we just met, I'm thinking I should wait at least fifteen or twenty minutes before I sweep you into my arms, right?"

"At least." I started my forward motion again.

We made it all the way to the parking lot without me falling over. So far, the evening was a success.

He pointed at a Dodge Challenger. "This one is mine." After hurrying to the passenger's side, he opened the door and held out a hand. "Watch the curb."

"Thanks for being cool with this. I know the crutches are a bit of a hassle."

"Not at all. We'll have fun."

I eased into the seat and buckled in. "Where are we headed?"

"I figured we'd play a round of mini golf, then walk down by the Alamo." If he was teasing, he was skilled at it. There wasn't a hint of tease on his face.

"I'm going to go out on a limb and assume you're being funny again. Did you grow up with sisters?"

He held up three fingers. "How'd you guess?"

"And you were the youngest?"

"Another good guess, but no. I have a younger sister." He flashed a wide smile. "I picked out a place close to here that's easy to navigate. We'll have a nice dinner and talk."

Harper seemed nice. I calmed down a bit, looking forward to spending time with him.

"Thanks."

When we arrived at the restaurant, his chivalry continued. "It's not the fanciest place, but I called ahead to get a table near the door."

"That was sweet. I appreciate that." I didn't dare look at him as I did my little crutch walk. That would probably land me face-first on the ground.

I held his hand as I lowered myself into the booth. While he stashed my crutches and settled in his seat, I surveyed the restaurant. From my seat, I could see four television screens, most of the bar, the hostess desk, and one other booth.

A menu hid the man's face, but his boots sure looked familiar. Did Zach intend to hide his face all evening? What kind of dumb luck landed him at the same restaurant?

Harper straightened his silverware. "Whatever you need, just tell me."

"How long have you been with the fire department?"

"Seven years. Adam and I started about the same time. That's how we met." He glanced at the menu. "Did you grow up around here?"

I forced myself not to look as the menu in the other booth lowered ever so slightly. "Yes. In the Hill Country, a little bit west of San Antonio. You?"

"Dallas. I moved here because they had an opening. I like it. Can't imagine leaving."

The waitress took our order, and I was feeling pretty good about myself. Here I was holding an intelligent conversation with Harper, knowing that Zach was probably hearing the whole thing.

"Adam said you're a photographer."

I studied the menu. "I am. I really enjoy it."

"How rude of me!" Harper shook his head. "Would you like to sit on this side? The view from here is much better."

Was he being nice, or did he want to check the scores scrolling at the bottom of each screen?

"Whatever works for you." I could be nice and accommodating.

"I'd feel better if we switched." Maybe he wanted to check out one of the hostesses.

After an awkward shuffling, I was sitting so that I could no longer see Zach.

"Do you have a gallery or a website for your photography?" Harper really was a nice guy.

"My gallery is just a separate room in my office. But I have a virtual gallery on my website." I rattled off the website URL.

The waitress set food on the table. I loaded my baked potato with butter and cheese. But I left off the green onions. Who wanted those on a perfectly good potato?

"I'll look it up after we eat." Harper cut into his steak, then leaned across the table. "Do you know that guy? He keeps looking this way." He used his eyebrow to indicate Zach, as if I needed the hint.

I ran through a thousand explanations in my head, trying to decide which sounded the least weird. "That's Zach. I've known him since I was ten." Somehow, that was the best I could come up with. "He's my older brother's best friend."

"That's not weird at all." Harper chuckled. "Should I ask him to join us?"

"You don't have to—no. I'm sure he—why would you do that?"

Harper patted my hand. "I'd like to invite him. But if you'd rather we not, I won't."

"I don't mind. But why would you want him here?" I knew all the reasons I wanted Zach at the table and had an equal number of reasons for not wanting him anywhere near me while I was trying to move on.

Harper stood up, then perched at the edge of my bench seat. "His plate has been empty since we arrived. He's had his coffee refilled three times, and I'm not sure if that's his second or third slice of pie. It's pretty clear that he's not leaving until we walk out of here. We might as well invite our chaperone to sit with us, right?"

Chaperone. It was obvious to everyone. "When you put it that way."

Harper jumped up and strolled to Zach's table.

I focused on my plate, listening.

"I'm Harper. Would you like to join us?"

"Thanks for the offer, but I don't want to intrude." Zach sounded so sincere.

The voices dropped to a whisper, and I glanced back over my shoulder.

Zach made eye contact but only briefly. "In that case, sure. I'll move to your table."

In what case? What did Harper say?

"Hey there Ca—Haley. How should we do this?" Zach glanced at both sides of the booth. "Harper, you should sit next to her."

I scooted over to make room. My phone buzzed as I shifted, and while Harper moved his plate and silverware, I checked my messages.

If you need to elevate your foot, you can rest it on my knee. Zach was maddening. And how had he gotten my number?

No! After hitting send, I tucked the phone away.

"Haley says you've known her since she was ten." Harper shoved his broccoli to the side of his plate, which was a mark in the plus column.

Zach sipped his coffee. "Seems like yesterday. She's grown up so much."

I kicked him under the table, and he didn't even look up.

"She's a great photographer but a horrible camper." He finished the last bite of his pie. "What do you do, Harper?"

"I'm a firefighter. You?"

"I'm an investigator in Schatz County. It's west of town."

"You grew up there?" Harper was nearly done with his food, and I'd barely taken two bites.

Zach nodded. "What do you want to know about Haley?"

"He thinks he's funny." I shot Zach a death glare. "We were talking about something before our food came. Oh, what was it?" I racked my brain, trying to find anything else to talk about.

"Your website!" Harper pushed his plate away and pulled out his phone. "Wow. This is some great stuff." He scrolled through photos. "This one with the hand holding the poker and tending to the fire—it's fantastic."

Zach dropped his hands off the table.

"Thanks. I like the way the fire danced in the air." Keeping my eyes on the screen, I avoided looking at Zach.

Harper turned the screen toward Zach. "Have you seen these?"

"Not the pictures, no."

I wanted to slide under the table. The early poundings of a headache thumped on my skull. I slipped ibuprofen out of my purse and tried to take them without the guys noticing.

Zach bumped my foot and raised his eyebrows. He was hovering more than my brother.

"Dessert?" Harper slid the dessert menu next to my plate. "The choices look good."

Zach gave his advice without being asked. "I highly recommend the lemon pie and the apple pie. I think this time, the peanut butter pie is calling me."

"Three slices? Really, Zach?" I pointed at a decadent chocolate dessert. "That looks tempting."

"I work out. I can handle the extra calories." Zach flashed that deliciously mischievous grin.

Harper caught the waitress's attention. "After all this, I'll have to run seven or eight miles instead of my usual five."

I was embarrassed for them.

"Can I interest you in dessert?" The waitress shot me a congratulatory look.

Sitting at the table with two totally hot guys earned me that look. "I'll have the triple chocolate brownie pie."

"Apple for me," Harper said before nodding toward Zach.

"I'll have that triple chocolate thing." Zach lifted his mug. "And a little more coffee."

If he had any more, he'd never sleep again.

STANDING OUTSIDE THE RESTAURANT, Zach tipped his hat to me, then shook hands with Harper. "It was great to meet you. I'll tell her brother that you're a nice guy."

Harper laughed. "I appreciate that. We'll have to do this again, but next time, we should double date."

"Perfect." Zach used the same tone he'd use when agreeing to watch a romantic comedy—sweet-sounding but completely fake.

I forced a smile. Between the pounding in my head and the throbbing in my ankle, I wanted to go home.

"You stay here. I'll pull the car up for you." Harper turned toward Zach. "Do you mind staying with her a second?"

"I can do that." Zach stepped closer as Harper walked away. "If you start to fall, tilt this way."

I waited until Harper was out of earshot. "You completely ruined my date. And I . . ." I wasn't sure if I liked Harper enough to go out with him again. He was good-looking and pleasant, but there was no zing.

Zach stood way too close. "Carrot, I'm sorry. I wasn't trying to—"

"What *were* you trying to do, Zach? What?" I blinked, determined not to cry.

"I didn't plan to be at the same place. It was a coincidence. I swear." He nodded toward the car. "He's pulling up. Can we talk later?"

"I don't think that's a great idea." I smiled as Harper jumped out and ran around the car.

He opened the car door. "Your carriage awaits."

"Thank you." Using Harper's hand, I slid into the car.

As we pulled away from the curb, Zach didn't move. I didn't understand him at all.

CHAPTER 9

*M*ixing Mentos and Coke always resulted in an explosion just as ignoring calls from my best friend resulted in a visit. Eve didn't care that it was almost midnight.

"Hey. Come in. I only have chocolate ice cream." I hobbled back to the sofa and picked up my bowl.

Eve strode into the kitchen and returned with a bowl of ice cream. "What happened? Why are you ignoring my calls? Harper seemed so nice when I met him."

"He's very nice." I adjusted the icepack on my ankle. "What did he tell Adam?"

"Was it Zach who showed up at the restaurant? Was he following you?"

"He's got to be one heck of an investigator because he beat us to the restaurant with enough time to eat an entire meal. He had no idea where my date would take me. It was dumb luck. But Zach wouldn't leave. So Harper invited him to join us."

"And?"

I shrugged. "How do you think it went? My date was

sitting beside me, and the guy I've dreamed about for almost twenty years was sitting across the table. Ugh, I sound so lame saying that."

"Harper said he thought your friend was jealous."

"I'd laugh but my ribs are still a tad sore. Jealous. That is funny." I held out my bowl. "Will you serve me a little more?"

Eve was becoming a pro at filling a bowl in under a minute. "Haley, you can't do this. Either talk to Zach and figure out what's going on or find someone else to dream about."

I wished I knew how to change my dreams. "He asked me if I wanted to go out again."

"What did you tell him? Poor Harper."

"Why can't I like guys who like me? What's *wrong* with me? Am I that stupid? He's sweet and hot, but—"

"He's not Zach."

"Maybe I need to give him another chance." I wiped my eyes.

Eve shook her head. "Don't do that to Harper."

"You're right." I flopped back on the cushions and nearly spilled ice cream all over the couch. "I can't force it. It'll happen when it happens."

"You should sleep."

"Because everything will be brighter in the morning?" I finished off the last of my ice cream.

Eve laughed. "No. Because you look terrible."

Honesty was the basis of all true friendships.

I stuck my tongue out at her. "Thanks a lot."

* * *

MOANING, I rolled over and buried my head under a pillow. If I ignored whoever was knocking at my door, surely they'd take a hint and leave.

But no.

My phone buzzed, and my brother's picture filled the screen.

"Hello."

"I have doughnuts. Open the door."

"Why are you here, Hank?" I rolled out of bed.

"Dooooooughnuts. I even got you some of those weird-shaped ones that are covered in chocolate and filled with that cream you like."

"You mean éclairs?"

"That's what I got. Are you going to open the door?"

"I'm coming. I have a sprained ankle, remember?"

"Excuses."

I limped across the apartment and pulled open the door. "To what do I owe this sweet surprise?"

"Can't a brother be nice to his sister without some underlying motive?" He set the box on the table. "I'll make coffee."

"Thanks."

"I invited Zach, but he had something going on." The coffee grinder drowned out the rest of whatever Hank said.

I painted on my happy face. Going back to bed now wasn't an option.

"We need to talk about Christmas. It's in less than three weeks. Do we want to spend it here in your apartment? Or at the house? We haven't spent a Christmas there since . . ." Hank took a bite of his doughnut. "Zach might let us use his house."

Since our parents died. The house had sat vacant for a while because neither of us had the heart to sell it. When Hank moved back from Montana, he moved in. But I wasn't sure I wanted to spend Christmas there.

"Anywhere is fine."

"I want some place where we can all celebrate together on Christmas Eve then walk responsibly to the tree on

Christmas morning." The more Hank talked, the worse it got. He acted like Zach was just another sibling.

"I don't mind driving early on Christmas." I bit into an éclair. "This is good. Thank you."

"I'll text Zach and see if he wants to do it at his place. I can help you get a tree for here though. You don't have a single Christmas decoration out."

I pointed at my ankle. "This is my excuse."

"Well, I'm going to help get you into the Christmas spirit. Finish up. Then we'll go shopping."

"Hank, I really don't feel like shopping or walking around. You can pick out a tree and bring it over."

He licked icing off his fingers. "All right. I can do that."

Fifteen minutes later, Hank left to get me a tree. Instead of digging out my boxes of decorations, I flopped on the sofa and closed my eyes. I'd been up way too late studying every detail of my boring popcorn-covered ceiling. Mostly, I replayed dinner in my head over and over.

I didn't blame Zach for being at the restaurant. He didn't know. But why did he stay? He'd taken treating me like a kid sister to a whole new level and at the worst time.

When I gave up trying to figure it out, I fell asleep. And of course, my subconscious dropped me right into Zach's arms in that field.

If I steered clear of Zach, by Christmas I would be able to deal with spending a few days in his company. Maybe.

Hank's knock pulled me out of a deep sleep. Wiping drool off my chin, I opened the door.

"What do you think?" He held up a miniature version of the perfect tree. "I thought a small one would work better in here."

"It's great. You're probably right. A big one would take up a lot of space. I haven't pulled anything out. It's in the hall closet." I limped back to the sofa.

"You keep that foot up. I'll grab stuff." He whistled carols as he worked.

Within an hour, my apartment was decked out for Christmas.

I shifted my feet so that Hank could sit down. "Thank you. It looks really nice."

"It's the least I can do. Thanks for putting up with me." He shrugged. "I know the divorce put you in an awkward spot."

"I still love both of you."

"I'm not expecting you to spend every minute of Christmas with me. I know you typically spend time with Eve, but I've learned that friends and family are the important things." Hank scrubbed his face. "That's why I want to spend my holiday with y'all—my sister and my friend."

Patting his arm, I smiled. "I know. This will be a great Christmas."

"It will be. And Zach offered his house. He even offered to cook."

For Hank, I wanted this to be a great Christmas.

Staying at Zach's would make the holiday torturous and embarrassing. But I'd muddle through. Somehow.

CHAPTER 10

*W*alking on two feet was a joy I'd taken for granted. Free of my crutches, I hopped out of Nacha's car. "Hopefully today goes better than last Friday."

"I know. Cami should be here soon. I talked to her right before we left." Nacha unloaded her camera gear.

"How's her car?"

"Totaled. Poor woman. She's had a horrible run lately. Her car had a flat and then got smashed. Her boyfriend dumped her. And to make matters worse, she's not sure how long she'll have a job because he's her boss."

"Yikes!"

"She only models on the side, but she's hoping to get more bookings. I feel bad for her."

Wind gusted, and I sneezed. "Dang Texas cedar. Every year, it makes me miserable."

"Take something for it." Nacha waved as a silver pickup turned into the gate. "Cami sure traded up. That's a nice truck."

"It isn't Cami." I focused on my camera.

Nacha moved closer. "Why are you being weird? Who is it then?"

"Zach."

"Oh." She studied her camera. "With this light, we should probably—"

"Hello, ladies. We got another call." Zach slammed the driver's side door.

I waved without turning around. "The owner knows we're here."

"You probably should have sent a memo to all the neighbors. They like to look out for criminal activity."

Nacha rolled her eyes before turning around. "Hi, Zach. As Haley said, we have permission to be here."

"Nacha, hi. I'm not trying to run you off. Haley was out here last week when I came by." Zach had a big mouth.

She shot me a look that said I'd be answering lots of questions. I gave another backward wave. "Well, good. If that's all you need, we're going to get to work."

The full minute of silence tickled my curiosity, and I spun around.

Zach stuck his hands in his pockets. "You have a minute, Haley?" He rarely called me Haley. What was he up to?

"Sure." Making a scene in front of Nacha would only add to the questions. I followed him to his truck. "What do you need?"

"To apologize. Can I buy you dinner and do it properly?" Why did he have to be so sweet when I was upset? He'd earned his spot in the doghouse, and I had no intention of letting him out any time soon.

"Apology accepted. No need to buy me dinner." I bit my lip, trying to decide if I should say more. Telling him that he made my thoughts a jumbled mess, and that no other guy had a chance of impressing me was not the way to end a conversation. And I wanted this conversation to be over.

Nacha wasn't even pretending not to listen.

Zach's fingers grazed my elbow. Even through my shirt, I felt the electric charge. Maybe it was static. The humidity was low. That would totally explain it.

"I haven't apologized yet." He stepped closer. "And you haven't looked me in the eye once since I stepped out of the truck."

Mistake number one: I met his gaze. Seeing sadness in those green eyes made me want to cry. Mistake number two: I opened my mouth. "I'm listening." If I crossed my arms, hopefully he wouldn't notice my heart banging on my ribs.

"I'm sorry I injected myself into your evening. Will you forgive me?"

I gave a small nod. "I don't want to talk about this right now."

He touched my hand, and another zing shot through me. Zach needed to stop dragging his feet. He was a walking battery. "Call me." Without another word, he climbed into the truck, then rolled down the window. "Glad to see that ankle healed up. How's your side?"

"It's fine." I shot him my do-you-want-to-die-slowly look. "You can leave now."

The get-out-of-trouble smile was back. "Bye, Carrot. Have a nice evening. Nacha, good to see you again." He turned his truck around and drove on his merry way, leaving me a mess. Again.

* * *

I TURNED up the radio while Nacha was closing and locking the gate. Maybe a really good song would come on, and I could avoid the questioning.

She dropped into her seat and turned down the radio. "What is going on with you two?"

"Zach still treats me like I'm the kid sister who follows them around and needs protecting. He ruined my date the other night."

"Zach did? He followed you to the restaurant?"

"No! We just ended up at the same place. My date invited Zach to sit with us."

"That was stupid." Nacha laughed. "The Zach I saw today was not looking at you like a kid sister."

"He feels bad. I should probably let him out of the doghouse. But what he did tanked my evening. It made it so much harder not to compare my date to Zach when he was right there." I'd opened up to Nacha a little about my crush on Zach, but it had been a while since the subject had come up.

"Haley, Zach was asking you out."

"No, he wasn't. With my date standing right there, Zach said he'd put in a good word with my brother. Interested guys don't do that, Nacha."

"What was that about your side?"

I would get even with Zach for letting that part of the secret slip. "I fell in cactus. But I'm fine."

"At least think about it, will you? Don't shut him out." That was gold coming from Nacha.

She hadn't spoken to my brother since serving him with divorce papers. But wisdom was knowing when to keep my thoughts to myself. I hadn't done nearly enough of that today.

CHAPTER 11

*L*istening to messages and deciding whether to call someone back wasn't ignoring people. That was called screening calls, and I did it all weekend.

Eve stopped leaving messages. Who knew when she'd show up at the door? Hank had called twice, asking if I wanted to meet up with him and Zach. *No, thank you.*

But Sunday afternoon, I let my guard down. When Hank called for the third time, I answered, trying to sound upbeat and chipper. "Hi, are you having a good weekend?"

"You've been ignoring his calls." It wasn't Hank.

I pulled the phone away from my ear to check the number. "Does Hank know you're using his phone, Zach?"

"He handed it to me and said to call you. How does barbecue sound?"

"Why didn't he ask me himself?" I pulled my hair into a ponytail.

All the tease left Zach's voice. "Because he thinks you're avoiding *him*, so he wanted *me* to try."

"I answered his call, didn't I? And if I say yes to you, he'd think you were the only reason."

"We both know that isn't the case." Zach closed a door. "What should I tell him?"

"Hang on. Someone is knocking at my door." I inched up on my tiptoes, trying to see out the peephole. It was useless.

"Haley, it's me. Open the door." Eve sounded almost giddy.

I obeyed. "What's up?"

Eve and Adam stood at the door, looking as adorable as ever. "We're going to drive out to the Hill Country, have dinner, and look at Christmas lights." She grinned. "Your ankle is better. You should come."

I was tempted. It would give me an easy excuse to turn down the invitation from Hank and Zach. "I don't want to be a third wheel."

Adam smiled. "Not at all. Come with us."

"I'll run and get dressed. Make yourself at home." I ran back to the bedroom, tossed the phone on the bed, and pulled off my pajamas. No judgment allowed. I'd had a rough weekend.

"Based on all that shuffling, it's probably good we are only on a voice call. A video chat right now could be embarrassing." Zach laughed.

I grabbed the phone. "Very funny. And I can't make it today. I have other plans."

"I heard you make plans, Carrot. Call your brother soon. I'll steer clear. I know why you're avoiding him. I really messed things up." He sighed. "I should go. Hank is going to wonder why I snuck off to talk."

"Zach, wait." I sat on the edge of the bed. "I'll check with Eve, but I don't think they'd mind if you and Hank joined us."

I had many talents, but staying mad at Zach wasn't one of them.

"I'll tell him. And thank you. I want us to be friends. I know I tease you. I've been doing it so long, it's second nature, but if you don't like it, I'll stop. *I'll try.* I'll even stop calling you Carrot if you'd like."

"I'll think about it." I ended the call and finished getting ready. Determined not to see Zach, I hadn't even made it through the weekend without giving in.

Giving up Zach was as easy as giving up sugar.

I didn't care what restaurant Adam chose . . . as long as it served pie. I needed a slice. Or two. I smiled as I walked back to the living room. "Thanks for thinking of me. Getting out of the house is probably good for me."

Eve squeezed Adam's hand. They'd already discussed that it seemed.

Lacing up my tennis shoes gave me a legitimate reason for not looking at Eve while I asked about inviting Hank . . . and Zach. "Hank called—would you mind if he joined us? He'd probably bring Zach along."

"The more the merrier." Adam smiled. "Do we need to pick them up?"

"They'll meet us. I'll text them the name of the restaurant." I buttoned my coat. "I'm ready."

I wasn't ready to see Zach, but I could fake my way through the evening. At least things weren't weird now. Having someone mad at him bothered that guy to no end. He just wanted to be friends again.

Buckled into the back seat, I texted both Hank and Zach the name of the restaurant.

Hank replied: *See you there!*

Zach responded almost a minute later: *Forgiven?*

For now.

* * *

Eve was kind enough not to ask questions. They'd all be saved for later . . . which reminded me that I was out of ice cream.

Hank and Zach were waiting in front of the restaurant when we parked.

"Hank, you know Eve. This is her boyfriend Adam." I pointed around the circle. "And that's Zach."

Laughing, Zach extended his hand to Adam. "It's good to meet you."

As our group snaked through tables, I fretted about the seating arrangement. Zach seemed so excited about being forgiven I didn't want to pop his bubble, but I also didn't want to sit beside him.

Sitting between Eve and Hank was the best option. I could make that happen.

Eve sat down in the middle seat on one side of a long table. I grabbed the chair on her left, and Adam sat to her right. Zach sat across from Adam, and Hank dropped into the seat across from me. I could not have planned it more perfectly if I'd thought about it for hours and designed place cards for each spot.

Adam leaned forward. "So, Hank, Eve tells me you're a paramedic."

Hank loved talking about the job. He lit up. "I am. I worked in San Antonio, then moved away. I'm working for Schatz County now." He stood and nudged Zach's shoulder. "Swap seats with me."

"Sure." Zach shifted to the seat across from me.

I studied the menu, reading over every item twice and still not understanding the words.

Eve leaned over to me as Hank and Adam talked. "You okay?"

"I'm good." I continued to study the menu.

She poked me with her elbow. "Look up."

"What?" It only took a second to see why. Inching my foot forward, I bumped Zach. "We're about to get a visitor."

"Haley!" My neighbor flung her arms open as she hurried toward the table.

Zach buried his nose in his menu.

"Lisa, hi!" I stepped around the table and hugged her. "What a coincidence! We drove out to look at Christmas lights. But we're having dinner first."

A boot connected with the side of my foot. Zach didn't like that I'd told her our plans. Or maybe he thought I planned to invite her to join us. I didn't.

"So are we! Lights and dinner." She motioned toward someone on the other side of the room.

The only guy looking at her was older, shorter, and had less hair than I'd expected. But he walked over.

Lisa hooked her arm through his. "This is Liam."

The menu dropped just enough for Zach to peek. That was his mistake. The motion drew Lisa's attention.

After glancing at him, she focused on me, daggers in her gaze. "You're here with Zach."

What I said next could only be blamed on what I call my little-sister syndrome. Doing things solely for the purpose of irritating someone was a study in psychology and also usually good for a laugh. Besides, why did she care who he was with? Thinking about how she'd tossed his ring out the door so unceremoniously, I rested a hand on Zach's well-toned, muscular shoulder. "Yep."

He clasped my hand as he stood. "Hi."

Liam looked up at Zach, and I succeeded in not laughing.

Lisa inhaled, her nostrils flaring. It wasn't a great look. "Liam, we should go."

"Y'all have fun. It was nice seeing you." I gave Lisa another hug.

She didn't hug back. "We'll talk later."

"Bye. Nice to meet y'all." Liam waved before following Lisa away from the table.

I stepped toward my seat, but Zach didn't let go of my hand. Instead, he rubbed his thumb across my palm.

He shifted so that his back was to Hank. "I owe you one."

"You owe me more than that. We'll settle up later." I tugged my hand out of his and smiled at everyone else at the table.

Hank turned around, watching Lisa leave the restaurant. "How do you know Zach's ex?" He turned his gaze on Zach. "And why did y'all pretend to be a couple?"

Zach picked up his menu. "Because . . ." He glanced at me.

Why did I have to answer all the questions? "She probably thought Zach wept every night after she dumped him. Now she doesn't think that. Anyway, she's my neighbor. I'm not sure if 'We'll talk later' was a threat, but just in case, I probably need to start looking for a new apartment."

Everyone laughed, and the waitress walked up to take our orders. Her timing was perfect. I quickly made a decision about what to eat while everyone else ordered.

At least my answer had appeased Hank.

I was the last to order. "I'll have a cheeseburger with bacon but no lettuce, tomato, or onion."

"Only meat and cheese?" She scribbled on the ordering pad.

I stretched up to see what she wrote. "And bacon."

Zach snickered, and I kicked in his general direction.

"What was that for?" Hank shook his head. "I wasn't the one laughing at you." How was his foot anywhere close enough for me to kick?

My aim needed work. "I'm sure you deserved it for something."

Zach nodded. "He totally deserved it."

I'd worried that dinner would be awkward, but instead,

we'd settled back into the same routine of teasing each other. It was comfortable.

Christmas might not be horrible after all.

* * *

ADAM PULLED off the road and parked in a gravel-covered area. "The light display is up the block."

The glow hovering above the buildings made that easy to see. "We can walk toward the light."

Nobody laughed.

I pulled on my gloves. "It got cold."

"You go ahead, Adam, we'll catch up." Eve tugged me closer to the truck. "What's going on with you and Zach? When did the two of you start flirting?"

Flirting? Hank hadn't acted weird, so I knew Eve was reading things into the situation. "We weren't flirting. We always act like that."

"Maybe I haven't seen you together enough, but what I saw at dinner was flirting, Haley."

"I think love has skewed your perspective." I stepped around her, feeling the need to run.

First Nacha and now Eve were saying things that would only give me false hope. I didn't need more heartache. I needed to think of Zach as a big-brother type of friend.

Eve laughed. "Maybe it has. But it really looks like flirting."

"I assure you. It's not." I wouldn't even know how to flirt with Zach. The art of flirting included subtlety, and I lacked that skill.

When we caught up to Adam, Hank and Zach were there too.

My excitement about the lights diminished because I was focused on second-guessing my every word and glance. I'd never been happier to have my camera. It gave me something to hide behind.

Click after click, I captured the magic of the lights. Over a million lights glistened in the oak trees surrounding the local electric building in the small town.

"Let's go talk to Santa." Eve tugged on Adam's arm.

"Go ahead! I'll get a picture." I changed out my lens.

Hank pointed toward the courthouse. "I'm heading over there to figure out what smells so good."

"We just ate." I couldn't believe he was hungry again.

"Zach, you coming?" Hank raised his shoulders, bracing against a gust of cold air.

Zach stuffed his hands in his pockets. "Nah. I'm going to stay here."

"Suit yourself." Hank wandered into the crowd.

I zipped up my camera bag. "You didn't have to stay on my account."

Zach shrugged.

What was that supposed to mean?

Adam and Eve clustered near Santa, and I clicked the shutter. "I wonder what they asked Santa for?"

Zach leaned close. "What do *you* want for Christmas, Carrot?"

I captured another picture of Adam kissing Eve before turning around. "I want a pony and a puppy and a—"

"A new doll?"

I swatted his arm. "No, silly. I want a place to live that allows pets."

"I appreciate what you did back at the restaurant. I'm hoping it doesn't cause you trouble."

"I'll be fine. She kind of deserved it after the way she treated you. But she looked jealous, so if you want her back, I'm thinking you have a solid chance." I pointed the camera at the carriages carting revelers down the street.

Zach didn't say anything.

When he tugged at the end of one of my curls, I turned back around. "Yes?"

"I don't want her back."

"Oh, good. Because you can do so much better." I needed to rein in my tongue, but my ability to keep silent up and left. "She clearly didn't. You're way better looking than that guy. Maybe he makes her laugh."

Zach tousled my curls. "Thanks for the ego boost."

"Anytime. That's what best friend's little sisters are for— ego boosts."

"Like when you'd go nuts in the stands any time my bat connected with the ball, even if I hit a pop fly that got me out before I could make it to first base?" He'd never stop reminding me of my embarrassing past behaviors.

"What are y'all talking about over here? First base?" Eve crossed her arms and raised her eyebrows.

Zach chuckled. "It's not easy to make it to first base. There's lots to consider."

Adam tucked an arm around Eve's waist and pulled her closer. "True. It's all about the angle and the timing."

I threw my hands in the air. "I know when I'm being teased. Y'all have your fun. I'm headed to find hot chocolate."

CHAPTER 12

wo days later, I learned that Lisa's "we'll talk later" wasn't an idle phrase.

When the pounding on the door started, Eve put her finger to her lips. "Act like you aren't home."

"We don't even know who it is."

"Haley." Eve whispered so quietly, I had to lean close to hear her. "With a knock like that, they are either mad or trying to sell you something."

I was much too curious to ignore the knock completely. When I dragged the stepstool into place so that I could use the peephole, the screeching sound could be heard two buildings away.

After that, there was no point in acting like I wasn't home.

I pasted on a smile and pulled the door open a little. "Lisa, hey." Opening it all the way might be interpreted as inviting her in, and I did not want that.

She crossed her arms. "Can I come in?" Her nostrils did that flaring thing.

"Sure. What's up?" I stepped inside and turned. "This is—"

Eve had vanished.

"How could you?" Lisa wiped tears off her cheeks.

Playing dumb never worked, but I did it anyway. "What are you talking about?"

"Zach Gallagher." She inhaled. "How could you date my fiancé?"

I could feel the syndrome taking over. "He's not your fiancé. You broke it off . . . right outside my door if I remember correctly. Am I wrong?"

"We aren't together, but I feel like you are taking advantage of him. You went after him when he was heartbroken. I'm only looking out for Zach." She truly had a warped sense of reality.

I was beginning to think she was less upset about Zach dating and more upset that he was dating me. He wasn't, but the idea still irritated me. I'd been dreaming of Zach for twenty years, but I'd never been accused of taking advantage of him. That stung.

Arguing with her was pointless. "Is there anything else you need?" I put my hand on the doorknob.

"What are you going to do about it?"

My plan hadn't really changed. I'd wake up every morning, reminding myself that A) Zach was off-limits and B) he didn't like me anyway. But I didn't want to talk about any of that . . . especially not with her.

"Zach is a big boy. He can make his own decisions." I sighed. This conversation needed a new direction. "But I'm so happy you met someone *worthy of you*. Liam seemed very nice."

She clasped her hands near her heart. "He makes me laugh. It was meant to be."

"Laughter is important." I was winning the conversation.

"I should warn you. Zach has an odd sense of humor. He's not very funny."

Now she was making me mad. I let the syndrome take over. "But he looks great without a shirt."

She gasped, then bolted out of the apartment.

I definitely needed to find a new place to live.

"Not that she didn't deserve that, but how would you know how Zach looks without a shirt?" Eve walked up the hall.

"You bailed on me."

"You answered the door. Now answer the question."

I crinkled my nose. "Would you believe it if I said imagination?"

"Not for a second."

"When I was at his house, he took off his shirt. And he looks very different than he did in high school."

"Duh!"

"Things were weird for a little while after Thanksgiving, but now they are sort of like they were before all that. Maybe I shouldn't have needled Lisa, but I can't stand it when she runs him down. I can't stand it when anyone does that."

Eve nodded. "I completely understand."

"What are we going to watch tonight?" I picked up the remote. "*Holiday Inn*, *White Christmas*, or *It's a Wonderful Life?*"

"*White Christmas*." She hugged a pillow.

I snuggled under a blanket. "Thanks for coming over. I wasn't sure how many of our Christmas movies we'd get to watch."

"Maybe I can talk Adam into watching one or two with us."

"Fine with me." I needed to get used to sharing my friend.

* * *

WITH THE PHONE tucked between my ear and shoulder, I hurried out to the car. "I'm almost done. I need a roll of wrapping paper and something for Zach." I locked the bags in my trunk before climbing into the car. "It's been a productive day. Still want to meet for dinner?"

"Yeah." Eve hesitated. "Adam's working. I thought about popping in to surprise him, but . . ."

"Go surprise him. Call me when you get home."

"Then I want to know why you are buying Zach a Christmas present."

I had a valid reason. Spending Christmas at his house and not taking a gift would be rude. "Talk to you later."

Not telling her now guaranteed she'd call me back.

Calling Hank as I pulled out of the lot, I hoped he'd give me ideas about what to get for Zach. "Hi."

"What's up?" Hank sounded chipper.

"I need to pick your brain. All my shopping is done except something for Zach. Any ideas?"

Hank didn't respond.

"Are you there?" I parked outside a store where I could get wrapping paper, wine, and candy from all over the world.

He cleared his throat. "Why are you getting Zach a gift?"

"You said he was hosting Christmas, right? Did the plans change? I'm always the last to know."

"What does that have to do with anything?" Hank was acting weird. "The plans haven't changed."

"I bought you a present, and since we'll be at Zach's house, I thought it might be considerate to get him something too. I'm not going to buy him a car . . . just something small."

"I have no idea what you should get him."

I pressed the phone to my ear with my shoulder as I locked my door and buttoned my coat. "What are you getting him?"

"The same thing I always get him—a bottle of tequila and a case of his favorite beer."

The word favorite triggered a thought. "Thanks, Hank. You've been a huge help."

In the store, I focused on my task. Finding wrapping paper that looked festive but wouldn't leave glitter all over everything was my objective. And while I was here, I'd get a bottle of wine for my stocking.

Stockings? The guys hadn't said anything about stockings, but that would be fun. I picked out two rolls of wrapping paper, then moved on to the Christmas décor. With a whole rack of stocking options, I could've taken all afternoon to decide. But a group of plaid stockings caught my eye. They only sold them in groups of two, so I bought four. Even Waldo would get a stocking. Each was a different plaid, but all of them had fuzzy tops. I could add a tag with the name, and they'd look great hanging above Zach's fireplace.

We'd need stocking hangers. Instead of trying to spell out joy or noel, I opted for Christmas trees and snowflakes. My next stop was in the stocking stuffer aisle. Some things could be enjoyed at any age. Kazoos, finger traps, miniature bottles of tequila and vodka—the age thing didn't apply to the bottled goodies. The alcohol wasn't in the stocking stuffer aisle, but it should have been.

I picked out a few international candies and a nice Riesling, then headed to the checkout counter. If I hurried, I could get Zach's gift ordered before Eve was done surprising Adam at the fire station.

CHAPTER 13

*T*apping my foot, I checked the app again. The last gift was supposed to arrive today. Tomorrow was Christmas Eve, so I hoped the package wouldn't get lost in the mail or stolen off Eve's porch. After provoking Lisa, I stopped having packages shipped to my apartment.

I didn't think Lisa was a bad person, but jealous women could be unpredictable.

Nacha leaned back in her chair. "Just go. You're making me crazy."

"I'll finish up edits tonight. Are you spending Christmas with your family?"

She sighed. "I'll stop by my mom's at some point. I'm not ready for the big family gathering on Christmas Eve. Tamales are great, but a hundred questions about what happened to my marriage isn't my idea of fun."

I gave her a hug. "If you need anything, call me. I've learned to take my own car, so I won't be trapped."

When I set the small red gift bag on her desk, she teared up. "And I almost forgot to give you tamales. I tucked them in the freezer."

"Homemade tamales are the best gift ever. You realize that's why I've continued working with you for so long."

"I know how to bribe you in the future." She yanked the paper off the top and lifted out the custom camera strap. "Haley, this is wonderful." She traced her finger along the pictures.

"I wasn't sure what to get you; then I remembered your ratty old strap that's starting to fray."

She hugged me again. "I love it. Let me grab your gift."

I peeked inside the bag. "Thank you for these."

"I tucked a little something else in there, but open it on Christmas morning."

"Seriously?"

She nodded. "Now go so I can get more work done. Merry Christmas."

"Same to you." I hurried out the door, eager to pick up my package.

Eve was waiting on the porch when I pulled up.

"I thought you'd be at work." I ran to hug her. "Where's the box?"

She pointed inside. "Aren't you coming in?"

"I want to go wrap this last thing; then I'll be back. I promise."

"We need our chance to celebrate since you made other plans that don't include me." She feigned a pout.

I picked up the box and hugged it to my chest. Of all the gifts I'd purchased this year, this was by far my favorite. Zach would love it. I knew he would. And that mattered to me way more than it should.

"You don't need me around. I'll be at your house plenty this coming week. We aren't opening the office, so it'll be hard to get rid of me." I inched toward the door. "Let me run home. I'll be back in an hour."

"Sounds great." She glanced outside. "Adam should be here any minute."

"Have fun!" I buckled the box into the passenger seat. There wasn't enough time to order another one. Keeping this bowl safe was paramount.

Back at my apartment, loaded down with my camera bag, my laptop bag, and the special gift, I fumbled with my keys.

"Are you ready for Christmas?" Lisa didn't hit me, so we were off to a good start.

I set my stuff down inside the door. "Almost. Once I'm done, I'll kick back with a bowl of snackalicious popcorn."

Her nose crinkled. "I've never heard of that. What is it?"

My heart thudded at the revelation. "Just something I had once. Merry Christmas."

"Same to you." She stepped away, then glanced back. After a half second, she shook her head.

Had Zach made it for her, but she'd forgotten? My heart wanted to believe he'd never shared his favorite recipe with her.

I slammed my door and grabbed the scissors. The popcorn bowl looked exactly like the picture. *Perfect.*

After stretching tape over the top of the box, I laid out the wrapping paper. My wrapping skills would never earn me a paid gig, but at least he wouldn't think a five-year-old wrapped it. I added a big red bow and set it under the tree.

I was looking forward to Christmas, probably for all the wrong reasons. But right now, I didn't care.

* * *

IF I DIDN'T KNOW my friend was in love, the mistletoe hanging from every doorframe would've given it away.

As Adam and Eve walked out of the dining room, he paused and looked up. "Oh! Mistletoe." He grinned.

The first few times were funny. After that, it made me lonely in ways I would never share with Eve.

"If y'all will stop kissing, we can open gifts." I checked tags on the pretty packages under the tree. "Mind if I let the dogs in?"

"I'll do that." Adam gave Eve one more quick kiss.

She beamed like a lighthouse on a dark shore. "I'll be in there in a sec. I need to grab one gift out of the bedroom." A minute later, she dropped down next to me. "I knew you'd shake packages that were under the tree."

"Whatever." I didn't have to admit that I'd already done that.

"Have you seen him?"

"Hank? Not in a couple of weeks. We've talked on the phone once or twice. I think he's having a hard time."

Eve shook her head. "I meant Zach."

"I haven't seen him since we all looked at Christmas lights." Going two weeks without seeing Zach felt long.

She handed me the gift. "Open it."

As she expected, I shook it. "It doesn't sound breakable. It sounds like a book."

An eye roll was her only response.

I tore away the paper. Life was too short to carefully peel away tape. She'd had a photo book made. The picture on the cover was from the year we first met. "You made me a book."

"You're my best friend. And even though things in my life are changing, that won't change. Ever."

"Dang it. You're going to make me cry." I handed her a gift bag. "You wouldn't be getting this gift if Adam didn't have a key to your house. That's all I'm going to say before you open it."

Shoving the colorful tissue aside, she lifted out the hand-made ornaments. "Paw prints!"

"Adam's dogs were pretty cooperative. Pookie was not. I

walked away with a few scratches. In general, it isn't a great idea for cats."

"I love them." She jumped up and hung them on the tree. "Thank you."

I pointed at Adam who was leaning against the wall. "He helped. Some."

"Only a little." He laughed.

"Let's open the rest." I sat down on the floor as the dogs trotted into the room. "I'm glad we did this. Now it feels like Christmas."

CHAPTER 14

$\mathcal{S}$tanding at Zach's front door, I convinced myself to knock. I'd never been nervous about seeing him, but tonight, I was.

My hand was partway to the door when he opened it.

"Why don't you come in rather than standing out here staring at my front door?" Why did he have to look so good? His red plaid flannel had the sleeves cuffed, showing off his forearms, and he had a Santa hat atop his head. "Merry Christmas by the way."

"Same to you. I didn't expect you to look so festive." I set his gift under the tree. "I need to get the rest of the stuff out of my car."

"I think this will be fun. I appreciate y'all coming over. Have you heard from Hank?"

"Not since this morning." I handed Zach the bag of stockings. "I'm glad we're doing this. I think he's having a hard time without Nacha."

Zach nodded. "What's all this stuff?"

What seemed like such a fun idea when I was shopping

now made me feel silly, but it was too late to change my mind. He'd already seen inside the bag.

"I bought us each a stocking. There's even one for Waldo."

"Please tell me you don't plan to stuff his with lacy, pretty things because I think he's given up his cat burglar days."

Instead of telling Zach that my pair of lacy underwear never made it home with me, I smiled. "Only cat treats and catnip toys. I also bought hangers we can use on the fireplace . . . if that's okay. I didn't mean to take over and decorate your house."

"All your décor will steal the spotlight from my single red candle, but I'll get over it . . . eventually." He bumped my shoulder. "Anything you need me to grab?"

"I've got the rest."

"Did you also get stuff to put *in* the stockings?"

"Of course. And I brought some groceries. I'll make a breakfast casserole for the morning."

He set the bags of decorations on the hearth and clustered the bags of groceries in one hand. "Help yourself. Move whatever you want. Holler if you need help." Leaving behind a whiff of cologne, he wandered back into the kitchen.

After a deep breath, I set to work. The red candle stayed in the center, but I added greenery and the hangers. Within minutes, four stockings hung above a crackling fire. "Come look. What do you think?" I studied the mantel, second guessing my decorating job.

He patted the top of my head. "I think I'm going to have you decorate every Christmas. This looks great. I'm finishing up dinner if you want to keep me company in the kitchen."

"Sure. What smells so good? Are you baking cookies?"

He shook his head. "I wish. It's a candle."

"You have more candles than any other guy I know. What's up with that?" I hadn't pictured him as a candle guy.

He laughed. "I own *two*. They were gifts. But this chocolate chip cookie one is my favorite. It really smells like cookies." Back at the stove, he stirred whatever was in the pot. "I'll throw the tamales in when Hank gets here. They won't take long."

"Oh! I almost forgot. Nacha sent tamales. Let me get them."

"Bless that woman."

I carried the two dozen into the kitchen. "Want me to put them on a pan or a plate?" I set them near the stove.

"I'll do it." He stepped in front of me.

Close proximity had my heart pounding. "Do you need me to move?"

"You're fine." He leaned closer and reached toward a cabinet over my head.

Inches from his face, I forced myself not to close my eyes.

He paused and met my gaze. His smile widened, and when his gaze dropped to my lips, my breath caught.

Reacting without thinking, I tilted my head back.

"Haley . . ."

If that was a question, I wanted my answer to be clear. "Yes."

The air sizzled as his lips were about to touch mine. But then he crinkled his nose.

Did I smell bad?

"Carrot! Your hair's on fire." He clapped my curls between his hands. "You leaned back into the candle."

When the sizzling stopped, he dragged me to the sink. "Lean back, I want to make sure the fire is completely out."

With his arm around me, I tilted backward. Having him run his fingers through my curls had my heart rate in rocket mode.

"I guess it's a good thing I didn't take hours to do my hair."

He turned off the faucet but didn't move. "And it's probably good you didn't have a headful of hair spray. You'd have gone up in flames like a dried-out Christmas tree."

It didn't matter what I did, I always found a way to embarrass myself in front of Zach.

He slid his other arm around me. "I'm glad you're okay."

I reached up and traced the lines in his plaid shirt. "Me too."

I think that maybe time froze because we just hovered there. Was he trying to decide? Was I imagining all of it?

"Hey. Sorry I'm a little late. I stopped to get hard cider." Hank appeared in the doorway.

Zach was on the opposite side of the room before I could say, "Quick, kiss me."

"I should probably dry my hair a bit." I wanted to thump my brother for his poor timing.

Zach nodded. "I'll get these tamales under the broiler. The beans are ready, and the rice is almost done."

Hank shoved a few bottles of cider into the freezer, then put the rest in the fridge. "What happened to you? Why is your hair wet?"

"I caught it on fire."

He glanced at Zach, then back at me. "How? What were you doing?"

"Being my clumsy self." I hurried to the bathroom.

Staring into the mirror, I pulled my hair to the side, trying to assess the damage. I'd only lost an inch or so. But it had cost me the moment.

I'd dreamed so many times of being that close to Zach and having him look at me that way.

After drying the ends of my hair and counting to a hundred, I walked back into the kitchen. "Where's Hank?"

Zach didn't turn around. "He got a phone call."

I moved and stood beside him. "Need my help with anything?"

"Nope. I have everything under control." He fluffed the rice, then fiddled with the knobs on the stove.

"Are you sure? Because you just turned on the empty burner."

He finally met my gaze. "I'm a bit discombobulated, I guess."

What was that supposed to mean? I knew the meaning of the word, but how did it apply? Was I making him crazy in a good way? Or did he feel like he was losing his mind and had almost done something completely nuts?

Before I could prod Zach for a better answer, Hank walked in. "They are down a man again. I asked them to see if anyone else was available." He threaded his fingers through his hair. "We going to eat in here or in the living room?"

"I set the table in the dining room." Zach slid the tray of tamales out of the oven. "Everything is ready."

Hank eyed the tray. "Nacha sent them?"

I hugged him. "She gives them to me for Christmas every year. We can't have Christmas Eve without tamales."

Zach pointed at the fridge. "I have some store-bought ones if we need more."

"This should be enough." Hank carried the rest of the food into the dining room.

I needed space to think. "I'll be back in a few. Y'all go ahead and start."

Slow deep breaths helped calm me. I strode back to the dining room, ready to face Zach again.

I stopped short when I heard my name.

Hank asked, "What was going on with you and Haley?"

I held my breath and pressed my back against the wall. Desperate to hear Zach's answer, I listened.

"Nothing happened. I was making sure the fire was out."

"I hope that's all it was. There are rules about things like that. Besides, you and me—we know that love doesn't last.

97

And what happens if y'all split? Where does that leave me?" Hank was so selfish.

It would leave him exactly where he'd left me with Nacha.

"You'll think you're happy, but then you'll make a mistake, and she won't ever forgive you." Hank was no longer talking about me.

"Your worries are unfounded. You have nothing to be concerned about." Zach's answer had an edge to it.

My purse was right next to me. I could grab my keys and be on my way home before either of them noticed. Tempted, I inched closer to the table.

"I thought about your idea. I'm going to suggest it to her tonight. I don't know why I hadn't thought of it," Hank said.

Thought of what?

"Good. And I don't mind if you let her think it was your idea."

A chair scraped the floor. The last thing I wanted was for either of them to catch me eavesdropping. I ran around the other way into the kitchen and smack into Zach's chest.

He caught me by the shoulders. "You okay?"

"Perfectly fine." I focused on the button halfway down the front of his shirt. That was safer than meeting his gaze.

He leaned down to look me in the eye. "Want something?"

The open-ended question left me tongue-tied. "Um, what do you mean?"

"To drink. Do you want something to drink?"

I nodded. "Surprise me." Before I could embarrass myself further, I rushed to the table.

Hank pointed at a chair. "We waited for you."

"Thanks."

Why did I always end up across from Zach?

He set three chilled ciders on the table. "Dig in!"

My festive mood had been replaced with one large knot of confusion.

* * *

SPARKS DANCED in the air above the crackling fire. I scooted my chair closer to the firepit and propped my feet on the limestone wall surrounding it. Shivering, I thought about grabbing my coat, but that would require getting up.

"Here." Zach tossed a blanket at me. "Hot chocolate?" He'd barely spoken to me since our moment in the kitchen.

The near kiss—because that's exactly what it was—caught me by complete surprise. Perhaps it had surprised him too.

"Please." I accepted the mug and let the warmth thaw my fingers before taking a sip. "This is really good. Did you add cinnamon?"

He dropped into a chair on the opposite side of the firepit. "Yep. It's Mexican hot chocolate."

Hank walked out to the porch. "They found someone. I don't have to go in tonight."

"Oh, good." It was awkward enough without Hank leaving me alone with Zach. "Did you get some hot chocolate?" I pointed at my mug.

"Even doctored mine a bit." Hank winked. "Listen, I know your apartment doesn't allow pets. I don't know why I didn't think of it before, but now that I'm living in Mom and Dad's house . . ." He sipped his hot chocolate. "What I'm trying to say is, if you want to move in—I know it's farther from work—I'd be all for it. You can even have your old room."

The conversation from earlier made sense now. "Um, maybe. My lease runs through the end of January, but I haven't renewed yet." I chewed my lower lip and braved a glance at Zach.

For a split second, he met my gaze, almost an acknowledgment of his role in the idea. *My Christmas list.*

What would I do if he'd gotten me a pony?

I wasn't even ready for a puppy. The list was meant to be funny.

Hank leaned forward. "It'll be cheaper than your apartment. It's paid off, and the utilities aren't that much."

"All right. I'll move in. You aren't home half the time anyway."

"Very true." He pointed at me. "No wild parties. I'll have Zach check in to be sure you behave when I'm at work."

Hank was either denser than a rock, or Zach was convincing when he'd assured my brother there was no reason to worry. Snuggled under the blanket, I concocted a plan to slip Zach's present back out to my car.

Whatever the situation was, that popcorn bowl would only muddle things up. I'd have time to sneak it out when I filled the stockings. But I'd look rude and heartless when we opened gifts tomorrow morning.

Ugh. I didn't know what to do.

One thing was for sure, I didn't understand Zach Gallagher at all.

He stood and stretched. "We going to do an early morning or sleep in?"

"As if that's even a question. Early. It's Christmas." Hank seemed happier than he'd been in months.

"I should throw the casserole together." I threw off the blanket and collected the empty mugs. "Mind if I take the sofa tonight? We're well acquainted, and I want to watch for Santa."

"I'm not going to complain." Hank laughed.

Zach shook his head. "There are two guest rooms. Don't sleep on the couch."

I stopped in the doorway and slipped into little sister mode for the first time that evening. "Are you telling me no?" I spun around, not expecting him to be standing right behind me.

He rested a hand on each side of the door and leaned in close. "That's exactly what I'm saying. If you watch for Santa, he won't show up."

"I'll think about it." I turned back around.

He tugged on a curl.

"What?" As much as I liked when he did that, I couldn't act like I did.

"Will you *please* sleep in the guest room?" His gaze dropped to my lips. Again.

Self-conscious, I licked them. "Only because you asked so nicely."

Hank laughed. "Consider that a win, Zach. She hates being told what to do."

"Oh, I know. She's a lot like her brother." Zach winked, then walked back to his chair. "Holler if you need help in the kitchen."

I'd never wanted to do a Tarzan impersonation until that moment.

But I fought the urge. Prepping breakfast alone would give me time to think. And I definitely needed to think.

CHAPTER 15

Staying awake until the house was quiet wasn't a problem. I doubted my brain would let me sleep at all. I kept replaying those moments in the kitchen, wondering what I could have done differently. Locking the front door after arriving might've made a difference, but I couldn't jump back in time. Because otherwise, I would totally have locked my brother out of the house.

Tiptoeing down the hall in my flannel pajamas, I stopped after every two steps and listened. When I was almost to the living room, I heard shuffling. I leaned around the corner far enough to see Zach tucking gifts under the tree.

Now I knew what he meant about Santa showing up.

When he dropped a small wrapped package into my stocking, I clapped a hand over my mouth to muffle my surprise. Curiosity would keep me up all night. I crept back to my room and hid inside the door.

After Zach went back to bed, I'd take my turn playing Santa.

Maybe he hadn't seen my gift for him under the tree, and no one would be the wiser when it stayed in my trunk on

Christmas morning. But being an investigator meant Zach noticed everything.

I'd still risk hiding the gift. What was the worst that could happen?

He stopped outside my door, and I held my breath. After a second, he walked on down the hall.

I waited an extra minute, then set about my task. Before stuffing the stockings, I picked up the pretty box with the big red bow and slipped out the front door. Once the box was safely in my trunk, I ran back to the front door. Coming outside in only socks was a bad idea. It was cold, and my pajamas offered little protection.

Eager to be inside, I reached for the knob. It wouldn't turn. I peeked through the skinny window next to the door in time to see Zach's back disappearing around the corner. Why wasn't he wearing a shirt? The house was chilly.

I needed to stop thinking about his bare back and figure out what to do. He'd locked me out.

Nothing came to mind, so I rapped on the door.

After a minute, the curtain moved, and I waved.

He opened the door. "What are you doing outside?"

"The stars are gorgeous tonight." I pushed past him. "I need to do my elf duties; then I'll go to bed."

He followed me to the fireplace, then scanned the room. His gaze landed on the empty spot where his present had been. "Everything okay, Carrot?"

"Yep." I rummaged through the bag of goodies. "If you stay, you won't be surprised when you open your stocking."

"I think I've had enough surprises to last me a while." He shoved his hands in his jean pockets. "If you get cold, feel free to adjust the heat."

I watched him walk down the hall, wanting to say something . . . anything. "Zach."

He whipped around. "Yes?"

This dance we were doing was draining my energy. "I heard you talking to Hank. He's probably right. And I wanted you to know I understand." I didn't really mean that, but it had to be said.

Zach crossed the room. "Why didn't you say something?"

"I just did. Having this conversation in front of Hank seemed like a bad idea."

"He's my best friend." He dropped onto the sofa.

I sat down next to him. "I know."

His fingers threaded with mine. "He's been like a brother to me. And you're—"

"Don't say I'm like your sister. Just don't." Things were weird enough already.

He chuckled. "Both of you mean the world to me. I just don't—"

"You don't have to explain." I traced the seams in the cushion with my finger. "I get it." And it hurt.

He lifted my chin. "If things were different . . ."

"They aren't." I tugged my fingers free. "You should get some sleep."

He lingered beside me. "I'm glad we talked."

I nodded.

Wrapping me in a hug, he kissed the top of my head. "Merry Christmas, Haley."

"Merry Christmas." I didn't feel very merry.

He walked out of the room, and I loaded the stockings. How had the evening started out with such promise and ended with so little? Wiping my tears, I went back to bed.

It was a good thing I'd hidden his gift.

* * *

I MASHED the button on my phone to silence my alarm, then rolled out of bed. The breakfast casserole wouldn't bake itself. Trudging down the hall, I mustered up my merry. Presents wouldn't take that long to open. After breakfast, I'd head home.

Home.

Why had I agreed to live with Hank? What did it matter? It wasn't as if things could get more complicated. And at least I wouldn't have Zach's ex as a neighbor.

I stepped into the kitchen, and Zach pointed at the coffee pot. "Want a cup?"

"A really big cup."

He grabbed a giant mug out of the cabinet and added lots of sugar and a little half and half to the cup. "Here you go."

"How did you know?"

"This isn't the first time you've had coffee around me." He refilled his cup but didn't add anything to it. "Did you sleep well?"

I shook my head. "I need to get the casserole in the oven."

"Already in."

"Then I should start slicing the strawberries."

He raised an eyebrow. "I'm not sure how I feel about handing you a knife."

"Then you cut them." I carried my coffee out to the porch.

If he wanted to flirt, he'd have to do it with Hank.

I dragged a chair to the far edge of the porch and gazed out at the mist hovering above the ground. For several quiet minutes, I sipped coffee. Alone.

The door opened behind me. "Your brother has his Santa hat on. I think we're ready to open gifts." Zach squatted next to my chair. "And you didn't hear it from me, but he texted Nacha this morning, wishing her a Merry Christmas."

"He rarely even mentions her name around me."

Zach sipped his coffee. "He talks about her a lot."

I wasn't sure what to do with that tidbit. My brother

opened up to Zach more than to me. But since I worked with Nacha, was that any surprise?

"I guess I'll cut the strawberries after we open presents."

"I took care of it. If we head inside now, we'll have time for gifts before the casserole is ready."

"Thank you, Zach."

"There's nothing hard about cutting strawberries." He flashed his wonderful smile.

"For being you and for letting me in last night."

"I'm still not sure why you were sneaking around in the dark, but asking isn't going to get me a straight answer, so I'm not going to bother."

"Smart man." I finished the last of my coffee. "Let me get a refill, and I'll be jolly as an elf."

He tousled my curls before leading the way back inside.

By the time I settled on the sofa, Hank was pulling gifts out from under the tree. "Haley, these two are yours. Zach, I can only find one for you." Of course Hank would point that out. "And these two are for me." He pointed at me. "We'll open one at a time. You go first."

Like a wimp, I chose Hank's gift. I tossed the colorful tissue in the air, then pulled two nylon sacks out of the gift bag. "Um, what are they?"

"The lime green one is a sleeping bag. It's a down-stuffed one because you're always cold. And the blue bag is a hammock. It's rated up to eight hundred pounds, so you should be good." He grinned. "We can get a stand for the backyard, or you can tie it to trees when we go camping again."

Zach pinched his lips together in an attempt not to laugh.

"Thank you." I'd never wanted a hammock or a sleeping bag. "A stand in the backyard would be great. Sleeping in a hammock sounds relaxing."

"I think so too. I'll go next." Hank unwrapped his giant

box, then stared at the small bag and card at the bottom. "Jerky?"

"Read the card." I felt a little bad for using such a big box.

He laughed. "Jerky every month is awesome. Thanks!"

Zach tapped the unwrapped case of beer, then pulled a bottle out of the bag. "I wonder what it is."

"No surprises. Same thing as every year." Hank turned to look at me. "Next."

I tore the paper away, but the box didn't give me any clues unless Zach had gotten me a case of wine. I gave the box a gentle shake.

"It's not wine, Carrot." He chuckled.

"That's probably a good thing." I yanked the tape off the top and pulled up the flap. I blinked and wasn't sure if I should laugh or cry. A little plastic pony had been transformed into a planter. And it had a cactus growing out of its back.

"Do you like it?" The uncertainty in his voice was endearing.

Unsure I could get words out, I nodded.

After a second, I pointed at Hank. "Next."

His eyes widened when he pulled a new fishing rod out of the gift bag. "Thanks, Zach."

I jumped up, and for the second time in less than twenty-four hours, I ran out the front door in my pajamas. I popped the trunk, grabbed Zach's gift, then raced back inside. Trying to catch my breath, I stood in front of him. "This is for you. It was in my car."

His fingers brushed mine as he took the gift. "Thank you."

"You haven't even seen what's inside."

"Doesn't matter." He tore off the paper and lifted the bowl out of the box. "I love it."

"Snackalicious." Hank wrinkled his brow. "When did you let her in on your secret snack?"

I was so wrong. Hank wasn't as dense as a rock. He was more like a boulder.

"Thanksgiving." Zach ran a finger over the word painted on the side of the bowl. "Thank you, Haley."

"I'll be back. I need to close my trunk." I also needed air.

I took my time walking to the car. With the sun out, the chill had subsided a bit. My heart was simultaneously racing and breaking. Zach had been so thoughtful with his gift. But it didn't mean anything. Not really.

Stuffing my emotions back behind the just-friends façade, I walked back inside.

"I thought the cactus would be funny. I'm sorry if you didn't think so." Zach didn't even seem to care that Hank was sitting right there.

It was easier to show how I felt rather than say it, so I threw my arms around him. "It's a great gift. I loved it." I pulled back and patted his chest. "I can't even imagine where you found that planter."

"I made it. I bought the pony and cut a hole in the back."

He'd scratched two things off my list. I was probably in the clear regarding the puppy.

"Well, it's impressive." I stepped away from him and lifted the stockings off the hooks. "Merry Christmas. You'll have to give Waldo his when you see him again." I handed Hank his stocking. "Santa showed up last night."

Laughing, they pulled out the toys and the mini bottles of liquor.

"Are you going to open yours?" Zach nodded toward mine.

I'd hoped to do that when I was alone. "I guess I should." I pulled out the scented soap, mini tequila bottle, and assorted toys. At the bottom was the little package Zach had dropped in last night.

I could feel him staring as I opened it. If the keychain

with the little puppy attached wasn't enough to make me cry, the gift certificate to the local humane society for a pet adoption pushed me over the edge. "Thanks."

He nodded.

Hank glanced down at his phone, and a smile wider than any I'd seen in months cut across his face. He nudged Zach and turned the screen so he could see. "Nacha responded for the first time in months."

Why did the perfect guy have to be best friends with my brother?

Life truly wasn't fair.

Thankfully, the timer beeped, giving me an excuse to run to the kitchen. After pulling the casserole out of the oven, I took advantage of the moment alone and unwrapped Nacha's gift.

The necklace with the book pendant was sweet. But it was the note wrapped with it that made me cry.

You deserve a storybook romance. Don't be afraid to live your fairy tale.

I wiped my tears away before the guys made it to the table.

CHAPTER 16

The sun hadn't yet crested the horizon when I parked not far from the barn. The neighbors probably thought I only took pictures in this one spot. That wasn't the case, but it was a beautiful location.

Magic hovered in the air. The moments before sunrise offered a serenity that I needed. New Year's Eve was a time for saying goodbye to the old and looking toward the new, which made it the perfect day for Adam and Eve's engagement pictures.

I still couldn't say their names together without giggling inside. When I'd suggested they take the engagement pictures in a garden, she'd nixed the idea.

They'd be showing up any minute, but that wasn't the reason I kept glancing toward the gate. Would nosy neighbors send Zach my way again? As much as I wanted to see him, it would be better if I didn't. My New Year's resolution was to get over Zach. Not seeing him since Christmas had helped me move in the right direction.

Adam's truck pulled through the gate, and I held up two

cups of coffee. Eve would need more than one cup before she was ready to smile this early.

As soon as Adam parked, he jumped out and ran around the truck. Instead of helping her out, he carried her to where I stood. "Good morning. We made it. Barely."

Eve grinned, proving my theory wrong. "He had to throw several pebbles at my window."

"And let's just say it's good that I have a key. The pebbles didn't work. I made her coffee and sent the dogs to jump on her bed." He kissed her before setting her down.

"The light is about to be magical, so grab a quick sip of coffee; then we'll get y'all situated." I checked my camera and made sure I was ready. "I love that dress. But if you need to do a quick change later, you can slip into the barn. It's not great, but it's private."

Eve bounced on her toes. "Where do you want us?"

"Right over here. Walk this way, stop, hug. Have fun. Adam, talk to her like I'm not here."

He clasped her hand, and they strolled through the field as light glinted on the top of the grass. When he leaned in and whispered, I wanted to faint. But instead, I clicked the shutter.

After several different poses, I changed out my lens. "Eve, if you want to change, now would be a good time."

She grabbed a bag from the truck and closed herself inside the barn.

"Are they turning out okay? I'm not always great in pictures." Adam dropped the tailgate and sat down.

"There were several that I think both of you will love. I'm not sure what you were saying, but she looks smitten."

He laughed. "I hope I do too. I don't want it to seem one sided."

"Oh, you look completely in love." I peered through the viewfinder, deciding on the next set. "If you need to change, run in as soon as she's out. I want to get more of this light."

"I'm only changing my shirt. I'll do it here." At least he warned me. "Sorry things didn't work out with Harper. Eve told me it was awkward."

I sighed. "That wasn't Harper's fault. He's nice."

Adam laughed. "*He's nice* can either be taken as a compliment or a soft let-down."

Eve peeked out of the barn and grinned. "Ready for me?"

"Don't move, Eve. Adam, walk toward her." The camera clicked as I moved to capture the photo. "Okay, both of you over there by that corner of the barn."

I kept them so busy during the rest of the shoot, Adam didn't mention anything else about Harper.

Eve hugged me before getting into the truck. "Have you heard from Zach?"

"No, why would I?" I hadn't even told my best friend about the disappointing late-night conversation.

"Just wondering. You'll call me as soon as the pictures are ready?"

"I promise. The rest of my day is blocked out to edit pictures." I checked my phone. "Y'all have a good day."

The truck pulled away, and I packed up my gear. Reluctantly, I loaded my car. Zach wasn't going to show.

* * *

AFTER SKIPPING lunch and spending hours editing, I couldn't wait to show Eve a sampling of the photos. I dialed as I stretched. "Hey there."

"If this is about pictures, I will make you dinner if you have anything to show me." Eagerness raised the pitch of her voice. "And you better be coming over anyway because it's New Year's Eve."

"Start cooking. I'll be over in a half hour. And I'm not done with all of them, but I can't wait for you to see these."

"I'm calling Adam as soon as I hang up. Come over any time."

I could've sent her a link, but I wanted to be there when she saw them. "I'll leave here in a few minutes."

Since they'd decided on a February wedding, choosing pictures was time sensitive. I planned to steer clear of Eve's mother until after Eve had chosen her photos . . . maybe even until after the wedding. Mrs. Taylor was a lovely person but could be a little tightly wound.

My phone rang as I sat down behind the wheel. "Hello?"

"Haley, it's Harper."

"Hi." I really hadn't expected to hear from him again.

He cleared his throat. "I talked to Adam earlier. February is right around the corner. Anyway, I wanted to get ahead of the game and arrange for a date before someone else filled your dance card. Would you like to be my date to the wedding?"

In my head, I could hear Eve scolding me, telling me to say no. And she was right. "Thank you for asking, but—"

"I won't make you finish that sentence." He laughed. "If you change your mind, you have my number."

"Thanks. I'll save you a dance." It wasn't like I'd have a full dance card that night.

"I'm looking forward to it. Have a good evening." He ended the call.

Maybe I'd develop a crush on Mr. Harper in the weeks leading up to the wedding.

I set my phone in the cupholder, then picked it up when it buzzed. If this kept up, I'd never make it to Eve's.

I hope your photo shoot went well. The dispatcher knows to ignore all calls reporting a redhead taking pictures at the barn.

Zach must have developed a sixth sense about when to insert himself into my thoughts.

We were there early this morning. And I'm really happy with how the pictures turned out. I kept it short and sweet.

I didn't have a chance to text until now. It's been a hard day. The somber tone wasn't like him at all.

I quickly checked the local news. The first article explained his long day. They'd lost a fellow officer in the line of duty. *I'm so sorry. Anything I can do?*

I'll let you know. Thanks.

Thinking about Zach, I drove to Eve's. By the time I pulled into her driveway, I'd decided on a plan.

I knocked as I pushed open the front door. "Hi. Do you by any chance have the ingredients for chocolate chip cookies?"

Eve opened her pantry and started setting ingredients on the counter. "Looks like I have everything, which is shocking. I like to snack on the chocolate chips, but I forgot I had a bag, so you're in luck."

"I need to make cookies, then take them to Zach. I'll show you the pictures while they bake."

She measured out the ingredients. "Talk to me, Haley. Adam won't be here for another ten minutes."

"Zach lost a fellow officer today, and I want to be there for him. We had a heart-to-heart at Christmas—"

Eve dropped the measuring cup and pulled me into a hug. "Yay! I'm so happy y'all figured it out."

"Don't cheer just yet. Hank made it clear to Zach that any hint of romance was unwelcome. So if things were different, Zach could . . . maybe . . . possibly be interested. But things aren't different. Zach and Hank have been best friends for twenty years. They've become more like brothers. I guess that makes me like a sister."

Eve backed up and shook her head. "Oh, Haley. I'm so sorry."

I shrugged. Wooden spoon in hand, I mixed the sugar and butter. "But I don't want to think about any of that tonight. I need to go over there. He needs homemade cookies."

"I think Hank needs to get a clue." She smashed an egg against the side of the bowl. "We'll figure it out."

"Please don't say things like that. I need to learn to be content with the way things are and not continue to hope for the way I want them to be."

"So what happened to your never?"

"I'd date him in a heartbeat, but it's never gonna happen." I pulled broken shells out of the bowl. "Smashing them isn't a great idea, by the way."

"Sorry."

"And tell Adam I'm sorry if I've made things awkward with Harper. He asked me to the wedding, but I didn't say yes."

"They'll be fine. I'll keep my eyes open for another eligible bachelorette to set him up with."

"I hope he finds someone awesome." I rolled the dough into balls, then dropped them on the cookie sheet.

By the time Adam walked in, we had four dozen cookies in the oven.

"Will dinner keep?"

"Yes. Let's look at the pictures." Eve grabbed Adam's hand as he walked into the kitchen. "Hi. Haley only has a few minutes, so we're doing pictures first."

"Fine by me." He sat down next to her.

I connected my laptop to her television and clicked through the pictures one at a time. Eve's grin widened with each picture.

"Haley, these are amazing!"

"Y'all are pretty stinkin' cute. I really want to know what he said to you when I took this one."

Her cheeks turned red, and Adam laughed. "We'll never

tell."

When the timer beeped, I handed over my laptop. "There are about five more. I need to grab the cookies." Heat blasted me in the face as I pulled on the oven mitt. I should have put it on before I opened the oven.

While the cookies cooled enough to keep their shape, I ran back to the living room. The last picture was my favorite.

Eve gasped as I walked around the corner. The picture of her peeking around the barn door was made perfect by the expression on Adam's face. The man was a natural in front of the camera.

She wiped her eyes, then kissed him. "I love all of them, but that last one is—wow!"

"That's because—you're wow!" Adam kissed her forehead. "Great job, Haley. Thanks."

"I'll come back when I finish editing the others. Probably tomorrow. I'm sorry I can't stay for dinner."

Eve shooed me toward the kitchen. "Help yourself to any of the plastic containers in the cabinet. I'll feed you dinner another night."

Five minutes later, I was on the road to Zach's. Showing up unannounced might not be the best choice, but it was too late to rethink my plan.

I ate three cookies on the way to his house. Tempering expectations and squashing hope required extra calories.

Counting to three, I pulled in a deep breath. Before I changed my mind and left the cookies on his doorstep, I knocked.

"It's open." Zach was clearly expecting someone.

And I wasn't that someone.

I set the container on the porch, but before I could walk away, the door opened.

"Carrot?"

"I thought you might need homemade cookies." I picked up the container and held it out. "They're still warm."

"You were just going to leave?"

"It sounded like you were expecting someone." I shrugged.

A door closed behind me.

"I am, but that doesn't mean you have to go." He pulled open the door. "Come on in."

"Haley, I didn't know you were coming. I would've gotten another order of enchiladas." Hank had the best timing. Truly.

Zach motioned for me to go inside. "Don't worry. I'll share. I may have cookies for dinner anyway."

"I really didn't intend to crash your evening."

He glanced down the walkway and kept his voice low. "If I'd known you were coming, I'd have planned differently."

Comments like that did not help me with my New Year's resolution.

"I'll only stay for a bit."

Hank smiled, but the strain was visible on his face. His day had been long too. "We don't mind you hanging around. You're a lot less annoying now."

"Thanks." Still holding the cookies, I walked inside, feeling a tad guilty for my irritation with Hank because both of these guys were dealing with the loss.

I rubbed his back as he passed me. "You okay, Hank?"

He nodded. "I will be. I'm worried about Zach though. He was on the scene when it happened."

Flooded with thoughts of the other possible outcomes, I stopped. Hank continued into the kitchen, and Zach walked out to the back porch.

I followed Zach.

He stood at the far end of the porch, staring out at the

horizon. He probably hadn't even noticed the pinks and blues painted across the sky.

Rubbing his back as I stepped up behind him, I set the cookies on a chair. "I'm sorry."

He spun around and wrapped me in a hug.

I slipped my arms around his neck and pressed closer.

Moments ticked by, and we stayed that way. This was why I'd come. I brought cookies, but I wanted him to need me. For a few seconds, it felt like he did.

When the door creaked, he let go and jumped back. "We should see if Hank needs help."

Had Hank seen us?

He wasn't at the door.

"Okay." I followed Zach but bumped into him when he stopped just short of the door.

"Thank you for coming tonight. It means a lot." He squeezed my hand, then walked inside. "Hey, Hank, sorry to leave you with all the work."

Hank gave me a look that said he'd seen the hug. Would he interpret it as comforting a friend? Based on his scowl, I guessed he was thinking something else entirely.

I glanced at my phone. "I need to run. Enjoy the cookies. And I'm sorry about what happened." I headed for the front door before anyone could ask me to stay. Not that they would.

Almost to my car, I stopped when Zach called my name.

"Haley, why are you in such a rush?"

I'd built a strong defensive wall, holding in my emotions, but talking threatened to put a chink in my wall. I shook my head. "Y'all don't need me hanging around."

"There's plenty of food." He stuffed his hands in his pockets. "Why are you leaving?"

"I thought I could make it better, but being here is only

making things worse. Hank gave me the death glare. It's been a while since I've seen that."

"He's having a hard time because of what happened today."

"No, Zach. He thinks I'm trying to steal his best friend. I'd never do that . . . to either of you."

"We're all friends. Why not stay?"

I trailed a finger down his arm, keeping one eye on the door. "Another time. But if you need anything, you have my number." Fighting tears, I climbed into the car.

Zach waved as I backed out of the driveway, and he stood there until I was partway down the street.

I probably needed to rethink my New Year's resolution.

CHAPTER 17

After moping on the sofa for an hour, I ordered a pizza, then tackled my dishes. I hated doing the dishes. And as little as I ate at home, dish-dirtying elves had to be sneaking in while I was out. How could I have made such a mess on my own?

I'd just dried the last pan when the pizza guy knocked. I tipped him well, hoping he didn't laugh about the single girl ordering a large pizza and having no one to share it with on New Year's Eve.

Before I took a bite, my phone buzzed.

A very cryptic text from Zach popped up on the screen: *You were right.*

I hardly had time to ponder the meaning because Hank called a second later.

"What are you doing tonight?"

"Eating a large pizza by myself. You?" I reminded myself that he'd also had an emotional day.

"At Zach's. We should get together tomorrow—just you and me." Hank wasn't great at subtlety either.

"Sure. Text me."

"Meet me at the house. You can choose which room you want." He hesitated. "And Haley . . ."

"What?"

"I know you were hugging Zach because of what happened." He hadn't really asked a question, but he let the statement hang in the air as if he expected an answer. "It would be weird if it was anything else."

"I know. I'm sorry about what happened. I'll see you tomorrow." I ended the call, fully prepared to cry myself into the new year.

A knock at the door interrupted that plan.

"You didn't think I'd let you ring in the new year alone, did you?" Eve lifted the grocery bags in her hands. "I brought snacks."

"What about Adam?"

"He's got plans with Harper." She didn't turn around when she said it, but the disappointment in her voice couldn't be masked.

I followed her into the kitchen and picked up the bags as soon as she set them down. "Don't get comfortable. I'll grab my pizza, and we'll go to your house. The guys can meet us there."

"Really?" Her eagerness was impossible to miss. "You wouldn't mind?"

"Not a bit. Take these, and I'll meet you at your house."

"Promise?"

"I promise." I tugged on my shoes and grabbed a sweat-shirt. "I'll be a few minutes behind you. I want to throw some things in a bag."

"You can have the guest room." She waved as she walked out the door.

I kept my promise. Five minutes later, I was headed to her house.

* * *

I pressed a hand to my stomach and tried to stop laughing. Never before had playing Texas Hold'em been so much fun.

Adam flipped over the cards Eve slid toward the middle of the table, determined to see what she'd had in her hand.

"You didn't have anything!" He gaped, somewhat deflated that he'd folded.

She giggled. "I bluffed. And it worked." Pulling the chips toward her, she grinned. "Another round?"

"I don't think we have time. It's only a few minutes until midnight." I was glad I'd come.

"Time flies when I'm losing poker hands." Harper laughed. "Let's crack open the sparkling cider."

"Then we can walk outside and watch all the illegal fireworks." I stacked the chips and nestled them back into the box. "Or does that make y'all twitchy?"

"Definitely makes me twitchy." Harper shook his head. "It's a horrible night for fires."

Adam opened the cider, and Eve filled flutes.

Fireworks exploded in the neighborhood, and Harper checked the time. "Someone has their clock set wrong."

Eve passed out glasses. We counted down, then toasted the new year.

Adam tugged Eve into the dining room where they enjoyed a few minutes of their own little private celebration.

"Happy New Year, Haley." Harper lifted his glass again. "Here's to a great year."

"I'll drink to that." I sipped my cider, then pulled out my phone.

Happy New Year, Carrot. I hope you and Eve had fun. How did Zach know I'd spent the evening with Eve?

For that matter, how did Eve know I was home alone

when she'd shown up earlier? And she hadn't asked about my visit to Zach's.

Only one explanation made sense. *Zach*. How did he get Eve's number?

I tucked my phone away and finished my drink as Adam and Eve walked back into the room. "This was fun. Thanks for not letting me stay home alone."

"That's what friends are for." She gathered the glasses. "Another hand of poker or do you guys have to go?"

"I should head home." Harper yawned. "But thanks for inviting me."

"And I'm not in the mood for losing anymore." Adam winked. "I'll bring doughnuts in the morning."

"Wow, Eve. Where did you find this guy?" I nudged Adam.

Her eyes twinkled. "I ended up in a horribly embarrassing situation, and he swooped in to rescue me. It's a great relationship starter."

I rolled my eyes, knowing exactly the point she was trying to make. But my embarrassing moment hadn't led to a happily-ever-after. It had led to a we-can-just-be-friends.

After the guys walked out the door, I dropped onto the sofa and typed out a text. I wanted to send something meaningful. But that didn't happen. I replied with: *Happy New Year. Thanks for looking out for me.*

He replied: *I loved the cookies. Thank you.*

I ran a finger over his response. "Zach texted you?"

Eve sat down next to me. "He did. Said that you might need a friend. Didn't tell me what happened."

"Nothing happened. Not really. I hugged him, and Hank got weird about it. So I left."

"You need to talk to Hank." She pushed up off the sofa. "I need to put the food away."

"Talking to Hank won't change anything. They've been

friends for years. I can't mess it up." I rinsed dishes and put them in the dishwasher. "But I'll be okay."

Eve hugged me. "I have a good feeling about this year."

"Of course you do. You're getting married."

"I'm talking about you, Haley. It'll be a good year for you."

I really wanted that to be true.

CHAPTER 18

*B*y the end of January, I was eager to move into Hank's place. Lisa had taken to ignoring me and randomly turning up her music in the middle of the night.

Moving away was more satisfying than telling her I hadn't seen Zach since New Year's Eve.

Living at Hank's, I had at least a possibility of seeing Zach from time to time. I missed him.

The last of my belongings were out of the apartment. Only a few things still needed to be brought in from the car, but I was exhausted.

I stared at the two couches in the living room. "I'm not sure this is gonna work."

"We'll sell one of them." Hank shrugged. "I'm not attached to mine." That wasn't a big surprise. It looked like he'd scavenged it from the sidewalk before a trash pickup.

I positioned a throw pillow to cover the gash in a cushion. "I'm not sure anyone will want to buy it. What a mess." Tired of unpacking, I trudged into the kitchen. "What sounds good for dinner?"

"Don't worry about me. Zach and I will grab something." He wandered down the hall.

"Okay." I wasn't about to sit around the house, or I'd make an entire jar of marshmallow cream disappear. "I'm probably going to run out and get myself something. I don't feel like cooking."

The new normal had reverted to the old normal. Zach and Hank hung out, and I wasn't invited.

As I walked past the door, someone knocked. I opened it. "Hey, Zach." Turning, I hollered across the house. "Hank, your friend is here."

"Ouch." Zach chuckled. "I guess I deserve that. Sorry I wasn't here to help with the move."

"We managed." I waved and continued to my room. In under two minutes, I'd changed my shirt and put on shoes. Hooking my purse on my shoulder, I brushed past Zach. "Tell Hank I'll see him later."

He caught my arm. "Carrot."

"Yeah?" I stared at my phone.

"Are you upset with me?"

"Nope. I'm good." I gathered my hair into a ponytail and looped a scrunchie around it. "Miss the days when I followed you guys around?"

"I do miss how things were. You seem . . . different."

Good. I'd been working on that.

"Have fun." Racing to my car, I wanted to leave before he got the last word. I dropped into the front seat and yanked the door, but it didn't close.

Zach leaned down. "Want me to close the trunk for you?"

One look in the rearview mirror confirmed my mistake. "Please."

"Promise not to back over me?"

"I don't want you dead." I flashed a syrupy smile.

Zach looked back toward the house. "I want us to be friends, Carrot."

"We are. That hasn't changed." Once the trunk had been closed and Zach was clear of the vehicle, I backed out of the driveway.

I'd lived with Hank a little over a week, and I'd picked up barbecue from the old storefront on the corner at least five times. With its huge smoker outside, the place called to me. But this time, instead of getting food to go, I decided to eat inside.

I pushed my tray down the cafeteria-style counter and ordered enough brisket and ribs to feed three people. I could always take home the extras. I skipped the sides but made sure to grab a banana pudding.

"Will this be all?" Was the woman at the register silently judging me?

Bottled drinks were nestled into crushed ice in a metal tub. I surveyed my choices. "I'll also take a Big Red."

She swiped my card and handed over the receipt. "Enjoy your meal."

"Thanks." I carried my tray to the dining area.

Instead of individual tables, several long picnic tables filled the room. What better way was there to spotlight the single girl eating alone?

I opted for a spot near the wall.

With my gaze fixed on my food, I devoured the ribs before attacking the brisket. Considering Eve's wedding was in a little over a week, I decided to take the banana pudding home for later.

Someone sat right beside me, but I didn't look up. I knew the minute I did, that person would become chatty. And I wasn't in that kind of a mood. So as a huge hint, I turned toward the wall a little and put my hand on the side of my face.

Less than a minute later, the person bumped into me. I scooted toward the wall, and irritatingly, they did the same.

This person became harder to ignore.

After two more bumps, I inhaled, ready to explode.

Eve giggled. "Can I have some of that brisket? You can't possibly finish all that."

"How did you know where I was?" I pushed my tray toward her. "Help yourself."

She picked up a fork. "You drive a yellow Mini Cooper. You live two blocks from here. And you'd sell your soul for good barbecue." She dipped a slice of brisket in sauce. "What he'd do now?"

"Nothing. No one did anything."

"Don't ever try bluffing. You stink at it." Eve nudged me again. "You need to keep me company. If I show up at the firehouse again, the guys will never let me live it down."

"Zach and Hank are out doing something. We could find something to watch."

"Sounds like a great plan. I'll get another banana pudding on the way out." She popped another bite of brisket in her mouth. "You taking that home?"

"Yup. You saved me from eating the whole thing."

"That's what friends are for." Eve winked. "I'll meet you at the house."

THE MOVIE *While You Were Sleeping* was guaranteed to make any day better. Engrossed, we hugged pillows to our chest as the leaning scene played out on the screen. Sighing wasn't optional or voluntary.

"Maybe that's our problem, Zach. We never learned how to *lean* properly." When had Hank walked in?

"Speak for yourself, Hank. I think I'm pretty good at that

move." Zach crossed his arms and leaned on the doorframe. He was right, but I wasn't about to confirm that fact.

I threw the pillow at Hank. "Why'd you sneak up on us?"

"You didn't hear us because you were too wrapped up in your fantasy world." He waved at Eve. "Sorry I can't make it to the wedding. I'm on shift then."

"We'll miss you, but I understand."

"Thanks. We'll get out of your hair so you can finish your movie." He sighed and clutched a hand to his heart.

Zach chuckled as he walked up to the couch. "Nice to see both of you." He tapped his hat on the top of my head. "Sorry to ruin your moment."

Hank thought that was hilariously funny.

Thankfully, they both left.

"Nothing, huh?" Eve shook her head. "I don't believe that for a minute. That man wanted your attention."

"No. He wants everything to rewind and be like it was before he almost kissed me. I can't do that. Now, all the banter feels like flirting."

"Because it is, Haley."

If it was flirting, that was almost worse. The conversation at Christmas left no ambiguity. Lots of questions but no possibility of romance.

"I'm going to unpause the movie. I need a happy ending."

CHAPTER 19

$\mathcal{I}$'d been over every detail of the wedding with Eve, but knowing exactly what would happen during the wedding didn't prepare me for how amazing the day would be. I stood at the front, waiting for Eve to come through the double doors.

Looking at the people would only make me more nervous, so I stayed focused on the main aisle. But when the doors opened, my gaze shot to Adam, then back to Eve.

My fingers itched to capture those smiles, and I hoped that the photographers hadn't missed either one of those magnificent expressions. Being the maid of honor made it impossible to hide behind the camera.

I spent the rest of the ceremony wiping tears and reminding myself not to lock my knees.

The whole room bubbled with happiness.

After Adam kissed his bride, he escorted her out as the guests cheered.

Harper stepped to the middle and stuck out his arm. "Here comes the fun part."

"I thought this was beautiful." I clasped his arm.

In a tux, Harper upgraded from good-looking to wow. He grinned as we walked out of the chapel. "That part made me cry. The next part is when I get to laugh. You'll love my toast."

"I don't want to follow you. Please let me go first." I'd written and rewritten my toast a hundred times.

"Sure thing. Whatever makes you happy." He tapped my hand. "I'll come find you later to get my dance."

"I'm looking forward to it."

He slipped off in one direction, and I went to fix my makeup. We only had a few minutes until it was time for pictures, and I wanted to look presentable.

* * *

MY TOAST GARNERED a few sweet sighs. Harper's toast brought down the house. I had no idea Adam could even turn that shade of red.

When it was time for the first dance, Adam held Eve's hand and led her out to the dance floor. She gripped his hand so tight, his fingers were almost white. Then they stopped in the middle of the dance floor. Before the music started, he cupped her face with both hands and kissed her.

There wasn't a dry eye in the place after that.

The music started, and I dabbed my eyes, watching Eve's happily-ever-after unfold exactly as planned.

Hair tickled the back of my neck. I wasn't used to wearing it up in a fancy twist. I brushed the errant hair away, then went back to watching Adam and Eve. When the song ended, other couples made their way onto the dance floor.

Showing up single to weddings wasn't fun, but it had been my choice. Hopefully, Harper would ask me to dance. Otherwise, it would be a long reception.

The tickling started again. Had the air kicked on? It wasn't that warm. The February weather was perfect.

I turned to look for a vent.

"Hiya, Carrot." Zach grinned. "I wondered how long it would take you to turn around."

I hadn't seen Zach so dressed up since my brother's wedding a year ago, but that suit and tie affected me the same way. My heart rate sped up, and my palms got sweaty.

"Why are you here?" It wasn't the nicest way to ask, but that was the way we always talked to each other. And it was an honest question.

"Eve invited me. I came to keep you company." He leaned forward. "The guy over there—that's Harper, right?"

I nodded.

"Well, he keeps looking this way. If he asks me to dance, that would be awkward."

"Zach, are you asking me to dance?"

"I am. Sitting here isn't much fun." He stood and held out his hand. "I promised Eve I wouldn't let you hide in the corner all night."

As soon as Eve returned from her honeymoon, she'd get an earful from me. I didn't need pity dances from my brother's best friend.

I crossed my arms. "I don't feel like dancing."

"Please. I'm not above begging." He grabbed the back of his chair and shifted as if he was about to kneel. Sometimes, he took his teasing too far.

"Do not make a scene." I popped up out of my chair. "I'll dance with you."

"Where is the happy couple spending their honeymoon?" He shrugged off his jacket and rolled up his sleeves.

I stared at his newly polished boots. "A cabin in an undisclosed location."

"Undisclosed, huh? You know where, don't you?" He

pressed a warm hand to my back and led me onto the dance floor. "Which of us is going to lead?"

"I'll let you, I guess."

He placed a hand on my waist, and I tensed.

"I'm not going to tickle you. I want to dance with you." He lifted an eyebrow. "Is that okay?"

I slipped my hand into his and rested a hand on his shoulder. "Don't wiggle your fingers."

"That would be tickling. I'm not going to do that. At least not right now."

For as long as I'd known Zach, he'd teased me, and I'd dished it back. We were used to it. The only wrinkle was, I thought he hung the moon. And growing up, he thought I was funny. Now, I didn't know what he thought.

At my brother's wedding, I'd dreamed of dancing with Zach, but he'd shown up with Lisa, and I was hardly teased at all that night.

Now that he was single again, the teasing was back in force. But after everything that had happened, I couldn't enjoy the back and forth. It was like licking a chocolate I wasn't allowed to eat.

"But they'll only be there two nights. Then they fly off to Mexico to enjoy a cabana near the beach." I tapped his chest. "But don't tell anyone."

"Mum's the word. On a scale of one to ten, how do you think Adam will rate as a husband? Will he be good for Eve?" Zach twirled me, then pulled me back again.

"I'd say a twelve. He's perfect for her. I don't think there's *anything* he wouldn't do for her."

"Really?" Zach raised an eyebrow. "Anything? Would he really have given up his dogs?"

I stepped closer and kept my voice even. Thinking about how in love they were made it hard not to tear up. "In his heart, he knew she would never have asked that. She knew what was important to him. It's part of who he is."

The song ended, but Zach didn't let go. "What if he couldn't have both?"

I shrugged. The question didn't feel like it was about Adam anymore.

The music started again—a slow song—and Zach slipped his arm around my waist. "They look really happy."

I put my hand on his shoulder as we move around the dance floor. "They are. I've known Eve since tenth grade. You were already away at A&M when she moved to town. I've never seen her this happy."

"What makes *you* happy?"

Somewhere deep inside, I think he already knew the answer. For all my attempts at subtlety, I failed miserably in that arena.

Before I could say anything—not that I had any clue what to say—Harper appeared next to us. "May I cut in?"

"I suppose." Zach let go of my hand. "Thank you for dancing with me."

"Is he your chaperone tonight?" Harper always went for the laugh.

"Something like that." I was a mess. Dancing with a strikingly handsome firefighter, I focused on the guy who was off-limits and not interested.

"Do you know where they are headed after the reception?"

"I think Zach is headed home, but you can ask him." I could play dumb when needed.

"Funny. I meant Adam. My buddies and I planned a little surprise. We just need to know where to go."

I shook my head. "Nope." The song ended, and I stepped away. "Wait, did you put Zach up to asking?"

"I only asked Zach if I could cut in." He winked. "I'm off

to beg the info from someone else." Harper wouldn't have any luck. "Can I come find you again?"

"To dance, yes." Only three people knew where the cabin was, and I wasn't talking.

I found a corner and watched Adam twirl and dip Eve. Cameras flashed. The happiness etched on their faces would forever be captured.

When the deejay asked for everyone except the single ladies to clear the dance floor, I stayed put. There would be plenty of others ready and willing to dive for the bouquet of yellow roses.

Hidden in the shadows, I figured I was safe even when Eve scanned the room. But when she made eye contact with Zach and he walked over to the deejay, I knew I was about to be royally embarrassed.

Before the deejay could call me out by name, I marched out to the middle of the floor and waved.

That earned me a few laughs.

Beaming, Eve turned around and launched the bouquet into the air. Instead of diving for the flowers, the group of ladies divided like the Red Sea, leaving me to catch the bouquet or get whapped in the head.

I scanned the room, wanting to see Zach's reaction, but he wasn't anywhere to be found. How had he disappeared so quickly?

Embarrassed, I held up the flowers when people cheered, then hurried to my seat.

The guys lined up to catch the garter. Based on the shoving, they seemed more eager to capture the prize than the ladies had been. When Adam threw the lacy blue garter, the guys dove for it and tackled each other in an effort to claim victory.

One of Adam's friends, a guy named Javi, stood and held up his hand. The garter hung off his finger.

I brushed away another tickle on the back of my neck. "Why didn't you go out there?"

"Poor Harper. He tried really hard."

I crossed my arms and didn't bother to turn around. "Be nice. He's a really sweet guy. If I had any sense, I'd have come as his date."

"You turned him down?" Zach sounded shocked.

I nodded.

He pointed across the room. "They're getting ready to go. We should see them off."

I wasn't about to miss the grand exit. Reining in my emotions, I jumped up. "I need to be out there."

Holding my hand, Zach cleared a path through the guests. Guys at the door were handing out sparklers.

The crowd gathered outside. Crackling sparklers lit the area.

I pushed my way to the far edge and held out my sparkler. Zach positioned himself across from me, and we created the final arch.

Ducking down, Adam and Eve ran through, but she stopped in front of me. Zach slipped the sparkler out of my hand just before Eve hugged me.

"I'm so happy for you. Tonight was perfect." I brushed happy tears off her cheeks. "Absolutely perfect."

She leaned close. "Too bad Zach didn't catch the garter."

"It wouldn't matter because I'd never date him."

Eve patted my cheek. "Never say never." Still beaming, she kissed Adam then gathered her dress and climbed into the back of the limousine.

The door closed, and they drove off into the night.

I waved until the taillights were no longer visible.

Zach stepped up behind me. "You may not realize it, but we're the last ones out here."

"Okay."

"What did she say to you?"

"Stuff that best friends say."

"Well, don't look so glum. She'll be back in a week."

"I know, but it'll be different." I turned to face him. "And glum? Really?"

"Care to dance a bit more?" He held out his hand.

"Because you promised Eve?"

His gaze dropped to the ground. "Why else?"

"Why not?"

Surprised, he looked up and smiled. "Good."

I slipped my hand into his and walked with him onto the dance floor.

Emotional, I danced entirely too close to Zach. He wasn't the only one giving mixed signals.

After two dances, Harper showed up again. "Hey."

"You already cut in." Zach pulled me closer and continued dancing.

I patted his chest. "I told him I'd dance with him again."

"What for?" Brow furrowed, Zach looked genuinely irritated.

"Because I want to." I stopped.

Zach tensed, then motioned Harper over. "She wants to dance with you."

Harper eyed Zach as he strode away. "I don't think he likes me."

"Don't worry about him. Let's dance." I didn't know what to think anymore.

"You look amazing tonight."

"Thank you."

"And clearly, I'm not the only one who thinks so. Why didn't you come to the wedding with him?" Harper danced us in a circle, then twirled me.

"Lots of reasons."

He waited as if he expected me to list them.

"I didn't know he was invited. He didn't ask me to be his date. And he treats me like I'm his little sister."

"He sure doesn't look at you like you're his little sister." Harper put his lips to my ear. "And he's not looking happy right now."

"It's complicated."

"That phrase is over-used. One-thousand-piece puzzles are complicated, but people still figure them out."

"In this case, it's more like a two-sided, five-thousand-piece puzzle."

Harper kissed my cheek as the music ended. "Don't throw away the pieces just yet."

What did that even mean? I walked back to the table, frustrated with Zach and irritated with myself.

Zach stood as I neared the table. "Sorry about that."

"About what?" I met his gaze. I wanted him to name his bad behavior.

"For the way I acted. I've been thinking about what I asked you while you were dancing with what's-his-name. And I do know what makes you happy." He pulled out my chair. "And tomorrow, you'll need a happy distraction."

I sat down. "I'm listening."

He leaned forward in his chair but didn't touch me. "I'll smoke a brisket for you. Best you've ever had." He checked his watch. "I'll put it on early, and we can eat about four or five . . . if that works. I'll call Hank and let him know not to make other plans."

Finding some other way to spend my day would save me heartache, but my love for smoked meat swayed my decision. "What time should I be there?"

His green eyes lit up. "Let's say noon. I'll have snacks. We can play games."

"Did Eve put you up to this too?"

"No, Haley, she didn't." He brushed his knuckles across my bare knee. "I'm excited. This will be fun."

This was Zach's version of getting the band back together, and I knew how well that usually worked out. "I'll let you talk to Hank."

"I've got it covered."

CHAPTER 20

*H*ank wasn't a bad housemate at all. He cleaned up after himself. The guy could even cook.

I stood at the mirror, trying to decide if I should wear my hair up or down. The ponytail said, "Let's be friends." Maybe my heart and brain would get the message too.

"Haley, you about ready? I figured we might as well ride over together."

"Coming." A subtle shade of lipstick finished off my casual look.

Hank didn't even seem irritated about having me tag along.

If today went well, we could hang out more often. But it would be easier to be friends with Zach if I had someone else to cuddle. I'd have to work on that part.

I buckled into my seat. "Good idea about riding together."

Hank nodded. "I wonder what got into Zach. He hasn't made a brisket in ages. But you're in for a treat. He seasons the outside. His briskets are tender and tasty."

"I can't wait." The aroma of barbecue wafted in the air as

we climbed out of the truck. "Smelling this for hours will be torture."

"Delayed gratification." Hank laughed. "The best things take a long time to get right."

Like a two-sided, five-thousand-piece puzzle.

Zach opened the door and grinned. "Snacks are in the kitchen. Drinks are in the cooler. Cornhole is in the backyard."

"What's the occasion?" Hank headed straight for the cooler.

"Haley's friend got married. It's our job to keep Haley distracted so she doesn't wallow all week." Zach swatted my ponytail. "Thanks for coming."

"It smells wonderful." I'd really missed being over here.

Hank popped the top off a Coke as he walked back into the room. "How was the wedding?"

"Beautiful. Everything was perfect." I turned to Zach to ask his opinion but bit my tongue when he gave a subtle shake of his head. Then I had to say something so it didn't look weird that I'd turned to face him. "I need something cold to drink."

"RC or a Big Red?" He strode toward the back porch.

"Surprise me."

He'd already done that. Hank didn't know Zach had attended the wedding, and based on that shake of the head, Zach wanted to keep it that way. But why?

After wiping down the sides of the bottle, he handed me a Big Red. "I figured we'd save the RC Colas for later when we break out the Moon Pies."

Zach knew exactly what made me happy.

Instead of hugging him like I wanted to, I pointed at the back door. "I'll beat both of y'all at Cornhole."

"Not gonna happen." Hank chuckled. "I'm the reigning champion."

I hung back, letting the guys go out first.

Zach stopped at the door. "You can't change your mind now."

"I'm coming." As soon as I cleared the doorway, I turned around. "Thank you."

"The day's only getting started." He winked.

His shirt smelled as good as the barbecue pit on the other side of the patio. I leaned in and inhaled.

Zach poked me in the side. "Are you sniffing me?"

I wriggled. "Don't do that. It tickles." I moved a bit closer. Using a whisper as an excuse, I managed another whiff. "It would be weird if Hank saw you tickling me."

"It's weird that you're sniffing me. You just did it again." He buried his nose in my hair. "You smell like honeysuckle."

"It's my shampoo. Why are you being so weird?"

"Come on." Hank rolled his shoulders. "Ladies first."

"You should get over there." Zach leaned in close. "Need a quick sniff before you play?"

"I'm coming." I ran over and picked up a beanbag.

Standing next to the platform, I wound up my arm, hoping to beat my brother.

Zach grabbed my shoulders. "Watch your step. If your toes cross that line, he'll have to pelt you with beanbags."

"Thanks for saving me." Hopefully, my sarcasm rang through.

My first throw was sheer luck. The red bag dropped into the hole without touching the wood at all.

"Cornhole right off the bat. She's going to make it hard to keep your title, Hank." Zach hovered almost as close as he had last night . . . when we were dancing.

Hank shook his head. "I'm not worried." He tossed, and the little blue bag landed on the wood, slid to the edge, then dropped onto the ground. "But maybe I should be."

My second toss ended up in the dirt. I missed the platform completely. I pointed at Zach. "It's your fault. You didn't grab my shoulders for luck that time."

"I won't make that mistake again." His green eyes sparkled.

Hank threw his hands in the air. "Why do I feel like you're both ganging up on me?"

"I'm being nice. She doesn't play as much as we do." Zach acted like he was going to poke me in the side but stopped before he touched me. "I want her to have a good day."

I wanted that and more.

Hank's second toss slid into the hole. "Your turn."

Zach rested his hands on my shoulders. "Good luck, Carrot."

My brain was busy chasing bunny trails, and all of them involved Zach. My mind wasn't on the game, but I threw the beanbag anyway.

I let go too late, and the beanbag didn't even launch in the right direction.

Hank never saw it coming. "Ouch! Dang it, Haley!" He slapped a hand over his eye. "Do you have any idea how embarrassing it will be to tell people that my sister gave me a black eye?"

"I didn't throw it that hard. It can't be that bad." I pulled his hand away. "Oh." How could I be so wrong about so many things? "Zach, he's going to need some ice."

"Let's finish this game." Hank picked up a beanbag.

I knocked it out of his hand. "You can barely see. I admit defeat. You win."

"That's not the way it works." He sighed. "But this really hurts. We'll take a short break."

"I'm so sorry." I felt awful.

Zach handed over a bag of frozen peas. "I haven't needed this bag of peas since we tangled with those guys down at the creek."

"Remind me never to eat frozen vegetables at your house." I handed Hank his Coke. "Anything else I can get you?"

"I think my dignity is lying out there in the grass. If you find it, let me know." Hank tilted the lounge chair back. "I hadn't thought about that day at the creek in ages. Why were they mad at us?"

Zach dropped into a chair. "As I recall, it had something to do with you inviting his girlfriend to join us for dinner."

"That's right." Hank grinned and looked at me. "He got mad because she said yes. Her friend was going to join us too."

"That's why we had two guys mad at us." Zach jumped up and strolled to the barbecue pit. "We did some stupid stuff back then."

Like a moth to light, I was drawn to the pit—not to Zach, to the barbecue.

He lifted the lid.

"Oh my goodness. That looks amazing."

"Tastes better than it looks." He poked at the coals, then closed the lid.

"How long ago was back then?" I shoved my hands in my pockets so I wouldn't accidentally rub Zach's back.

"Before Nacha." Hank stared off into the distance. "I was a better person after she showed up."

I'd taken Hank's silence as bitterness, but I was wrong.

Zach placed a hand on my hip and whispered in my ear. "He's crazy about her. Some people are meant to be together."

"I wish I knew how to fix it." I leaned into his hand, ignoring the warning bells going off in my head.

"Only they can fix it. We can't fix their mess; we can only work on ours."

Ours?

I whipped around to face him. Had I stepped into a parallel universe?

"Whoa. That ponytail is lethal. You almost hit me with it." He patted my hip. "Let's go back over there. Your brother will feel left out if I only talk to you."

Whatever was going on would probably make my brother hate me, but it felt like sliding into a pair of well-worn jeans just out of the dryer. Warm and comfortable.

"Tell me about what other trouble you guys got into." I sipped my Big Red.

Hank pulled the ice pack off his face. "I plead the fifth. This is feeling better. Let's finish our game."

"Hank, I said you won. We don't have to finish."

"Getting a black eye from my sister is bad enough. Having my sister let me win is intolerable." He pointed at the Cornhole game. "It's my turn. And no more rubbing her shoulders for luck. I might lose an eye if you keep that up."

So much for thinking Hank wasn't bothered by the extra attention Zach was showing me.

"Don't be sore, Hank." I kicked Zach's shoe as I passed him. "I think I made him mad."

"It might've been me." He followed me out to the grass.

Hank landed another bag on the board, near the hole. "I'm ahead."

I picked up another beanbag. "All right. Let's see if I can tie this up."

"If you win, I'll watch a romantic comedy with you." Zach winked. "Your choice."

Maybe I was dreaming. If I was, it was a really good dream. "You're distracting me."

"I was trying to motivate you." He stepped closer. "Will *leaning* bring you luck?"

"Quit the jabber and take your turn." Hank pointed at Zach, then pointed at a chair. "Leave her alone."

I mentally calculated the distance between me and the hole, accounted for the wind speed—who was I kidding? I flung my beanbag into the air, praying that it wouldn't land in the grass.

When it landed in the hole, I jumped up and down, clapping.

"Don't celebrate. It's my turn. You haven't won yet."

"Yet." I flashed my best little-sister smile.

His beanbag landed on the wood, then slid until it hung off the edge.

"Sorry. No point." I kicked it off. "You know what that means?"

"Now we switch sides." Hank had always been a bit competitive, but this was taking it to a whole new level.

"It's just a game, Hank."

"It's your turn." He kicked the board. "Throw."

Indulging his madness, I tossed the beanbag. It landed on the board.

He landed his on the board.

As tempted as I was to throw long and miss the board completely, I knew he'd only get mad that I was letting him win. My second toss landed on the board.

Everything I did, he matched it.

On my last throw, the beanbag slid off the edge.

Hank grinned. "Too bad." He landed it in the hole. "Now we go back to that side."

Zach looked wholly uncomfortable. And he should because in some warped sense, he was the prize.

The game went on and on. Back and forth, we stayed close in points. When it was time for my last throw, I needed to get one in the hole to win.

I glanced at Zach, and he gave a small nod.

After a deep breath, I launched the beanbag. It landed on the board, knocked Hank's beanbag into the hole, then slid off the back of the board.

I smiled. "Good game, Hank."

"Thanks for playing." At least he wasn't a sore winner. "Zach, can I talk to you inside?"

Maybe I thought that too soon.

I walked around the Cornhole game, picking up beanbags.

After ten minutes, Zach walked back out to the patio. "We still have another couple of hours until the brisket is ready. Want something? I have chips and queso, and just for you, I made a veggie tray."

"Very funny." I brushed past him as I walked inside but stopped to sniff his shirt. "You smell like that brisket."

"You like that, huh?"

"A lot. And queso sounds good."

Zach handed me a plate. "Hank had to leave."

"Do I want to know why?"

"Probably not." Zach piled carrots on his plate. "Let's watch a movie."

"But I lost." I drenched my chips in queso.

"Would you rather play Cornhole against me?"

I'd had my fill of Cornhole for the short term. "No. That game left me scarred."

He didn't laugh. "I'm sorry about that."

"I'll live."

We settled on the sofa, and he searched up a movie.

"Do you really have a cat? I never see him." I popped a chip in my mouth, trying not to drip queso on my shirt.

"He's around. Waldo is funny that way. He's hard to find if you go looking for him." He clicked play. "This one looks funny."

After all the flirting, I was tempted to snuggle up next to him. But I didn't. I nestled into one end of the couch. If he wanted to snuggle, he could make that move.

He didn't.

We made it through the whole movie without me crawling into his lap or resting my head on his shoulder.

"That was funny." Zach pushed up off the sofa and held out his hand. "Brisket's probably ready."

I let him help me up. Instead of letting go of my hand once I was on my feet, he kept hold of it as we walked out to the barbecue pit. It felt so right, but I needed him to be up front with me. What had changed since Christmas?

* * *

FLAMES DANCED IN THE FIREPIT. How did I keep ending up on this patio with Zach?

"It's late. I should go." I stood, determined to make it out the door.

"I'll walk you out." His fingers brushed my arm. "Has it been a good day?"

"I've had a great time." No part of that was a lie. Despite the weird competitiveness from my brother, it had been a really good day.

Zach smiled. "I've enjoyed it too."

I sniffed his shirt again, not even pretending that I wasn't. "I'm soaking it up before I have to leave. That's one of the best smells ever."

In one swift motion, Zach yanked off his shirt. "Here. Take it with you."

Blinking, I stared at the shirt in his hand. "Go home, Zach. You're drunk."

"I am home, and you know I'm not drunk. Why do you look so shocked?"

"I expected that maybe you'd send home leftovers . . . not rip your shirt off."

He rested his hands on the doorframe and leaned toward

me. "There's lots of brisket left over. Come back any day, and you can have some."

I didn't know what to do with this version of Zach. I wanted to throw my arms around his neck and kiss him until I couldn't breathe. But I wasn't sure that was an option.

I seriously needed to sort out my thoughts. "What happened to Hank?" I reached for the shirt. I did love the smell of brisket.

Zach chewed his bottom lip a second. "We talked, and he's upset with me. That's why he didn't stay."

In all the years they'd been friends, fights and arguments between them were almost unheard of.

"What's going on?" I needed a bit of clarity.

"He says I'm being reckless. And maybe I am."

"What are you talking about?"

Zach leaned down and pressed his lips to mine. As much as I wanted to return the kiss, shock rendered me motionless. Thoughts were like a slurry in my brain—mixed up and slow.

He stepped back, and his shoulders slumped. He folded his arms over that bare chest. "Sorry. I thought—Did I misread you?"

"Oh no. Your reading skills are exceptional. I just thought —I thought I'd been writing in invisible ink. I gotta go." I'd spent too many years squashing my attraction to this guy. I didn't know what to do. "I have to think." I hugged the shirt to my chest and turned to go.

Zach clasped my arm. "Haley." Confusion, amusement, and something else swirled in his green eyes.

And that something else turned my brain to mush. Every dream I'd ever had about kissing him thundered in my head.

I launched at him, flung my arms around his neck, and snagged his lips with mine. Chuckling, he pulled me off my feet, and I snaked my legs around his waist. He put his hands on—never mind where. Suffice it to say, he was the only thing keeping my backside from hitting the ground.

I pulled back far enough to speak. "Zach."

He pressed back in for another kiss. "Mmm?"

"Don't drop me."

A laugh rumbled in his chest, and he spun me around. With my back pressed to the wall, his hands moved up to my waist. "Wouldn't dream of it."

All the little tugs on my curls, all the leans, and the teasing —he'd been flirting. Thanksgiving had flipped everything upside down.

As I toyed with the short hairs at the nape of his neck, he brushed his lower lip across mine before pressing in again. After several minutes, we came up for air.

"Now we're talking." He grinned as he eased me back down to the floor.

Clarity of thought wasn't possible anywhere near Zach Gallagher, especially when he wasn't wearing a shirt.

I picked up the smoke-infused shirt, which had fallen to the floor mid-kiss. "No, we aren't talking. I'm not ready for that. But that kiss will help me think." I spun toward the door and inhaled before pushing it open.

Behind me, Zach tugged at the end of a curl. "If you want more brisket, you know where to come."

I couldn't resist a quick look. "Brisket?"

He blew me a kiss. "I'll be here when you want to talk or if you need more help thinking."

I nodded, then ran to the driveway. I'd ridden with Hank, and he was gone. Why couldn't I have remembered that earlier?

Zach laughed. "I'll grab my keys."

So much for my grand exit.

CHAPTER 21

*D*elicious smells wafted from the kitchen. If this was how Hank displayed his anger, this wouldn't be too difficult.

"Good morning." I filled my favorite mug with the perfect blend of coffee, cream, and sugar. "What smells so good?"

"My breakfast." He shoveled some sort of scramble onto a plate.

If he was going to make yummy food and not share, I might have to find a new place to live.

"Help yourself. There's plenty." He handed me the spoon. "I can't believe you didn't bring any brisket home. I tore through the fridge this morning, looking for some."

"Zach said to come over whenever if we want some."

At the mention of Zach's name, Hank inhaled sharply. "I thought—you know what—never mind. You're an adult. He's an adult. I'm not going to get in the middle of it."

"I appreciate that."

"I'm really disappointed . . . in Zach. You've been after him, chasing him since day one." Hank refilled his mug.

Coffee splashed as I set my cup on the counter. Biting my

tongue and fighting tears, I grabbed my keys and stomped out of the house.

I wanted to talk to my best friend, but no way was I going to interrupt her honeymoon to vent. Not sure where to go, I called Nacha. "Hey. You busy?"

"What's up?"

"Feel like grabbing something to eat?" I couldn't exactly vent to Nacha about Hank. Or could I?

She knew Hank as well as I did. Maybe better.

"Sure. Is everything okay?"

"I need some advice about Hank. If that makes you uncomfortable, I understand." I held my breath, hoping she wouldn't back out.

Her keys jingled. "Tell me where to meet you."

Twenty minutes later, we were seated in a booth, and over a massive stack of pancakes, I told Nacha all about Thanksgiving, Christmas, the wedding, and the barbecue.

She never interrupted.

Then I told her what Hank had said this morning and ended my story by taking another bite of my pancakes.

Nacha reached across the table and patted my hand. "You can move in with me. I have an extra bedroom."

"That's not really what this is about. He's my brother. If I follow my heart, I'll be tearing apart what little family I have left. I'm not sure I can do that." I popped the last bite of bacon in my mouth, wishing I'd ordered extra.

She gave me a knowing smile. "I'm not suggesting you move in permanently, just while you think about it. You need to choose what's best *for you*. Hank has trouble admitting when he's wrong. Anyone who loves him knows that."

While this was definitely not the time to bring it up, the phrase loves him made me think she still did. Why wouldn't she talk to him? But as Zach said, that was their complicated puzzle to solve.

"But it's not only *my* relationship with Hank that I'm worried about." I pointed at Nacha's last slice of bacon. "Are you going to eat that?"

"Have at it. Don't be rash. If Zach is serious, he'll wait."

I nodded. "If I stay at your house, it's too easy for Hank. If I'm going to turn Zach down, Hank will have to live with the aftermath."

Her brow furrowed, but she laughed. "He doesn't handle tears well."

"He'll get a lot of practice." I finished the last of my coffee. "Thanks for listening."

"Please think about your decision. Give it a few days before talking to Zach."

"I will."

* * *

For days, Hank and I didn't speak. The time I spent at home was mostly spent in my room. I shed more tears than I had in all the last year. The torturous silence would end if I simply told Zach it wouldn't work.

But I hadn't convinced myself to do that.

If Hank and I happened into the same room at the same time, I left. Life was easier when he went on shift. But when his shift was over, the strain returned.

After work, I headed home, knowing Hank was off work. When I arrived at the house, it smelled like a Mexican restaurant.

"Dinner is ready. I made stuff for tacos. There are flour tortillas if you prefer soft and crispy corn shells if you like that better. And then on the stove, there's taco meat in one pan and shredded chicken in the other." Hank tossed a dish towel over his shoulder. "Want me to make you a plate?"

"I'm not hungry." That was a lie, but I wasn't going to eat right now.

Eve always accused me of equating food with love. Clearly, that idea ran in the family.

I trudged down the hall and closed myself in my room. It wasn't just the choice I had to make that bothered me. My brother's words still rattled around in my head and made me feel desperate and stupid.

A half hour later, the front door closed. I peeked through the blinds. Hank backed out of the driveway. Since he was gone, I wandered into the kitchen and helped myself to tacos.

Eventually we'd have to talk about it. Like adults. But first, we had to get past the battling-like-siblings stage.

I was stuffing the second taco in my mouth when Hank came home.

"Are we going to ignore each other, or do you want to talk about it?"

"Talk about what?" I downed half my Topo Chico.

"Haley, don't be stubborn." The man wasn't doing himself any favors. "Am I wrong? Tell me if I'm being an idiot."

The invitation was too good to pass up. "You're being an idiot."

Hank flung his arms wide. "Do you even know why I'm mad?"

"No, actually. I have a general idea, but I don't know specifics." I rinsed my plate and put it in the dishwasher. "So please tell me."

"I pulled Zach aside and told him that it looked as if he was flirting with you." Hank dragged his fingers through his hair. "Do you know what he said to me?"

I shook my head.

"He said that he was and that he thought it was working. Can you believe that? He didn't even ask my opinion."

Struggling not to laugh, I opened the fridge, pretending to look for something. "Well, what was your opinion? Did you think it was working?"

"Fine. Laugh. I'm trying to be adult about this."

"Do you realize how childish you're being? You aren't the only one who considers Zach a friend. Do you feel the need to approve of everyone he wants to date? Does my opinion count for anything?"

"You're my sister. If he says something awful to you or breaks your heart, I'm required to be mad, but he's my best friend."

"You mean something awful like accusing me of chasing him?"

"I was mad."

"I know." I rubbed my temples. "I'm not sure talking about it is helping."

"I don't want you to be mad at me." He held open his arms. "Please."

It was just like him to sound sweet and act as if he was apologizing, but he wasn't. Nothing had changed.

But I would look like the meanie if I walked away angry. I hugged him. "You're my brother. Nothing will change that." Non-apologies ran in the family.

"I'm glad we sorted that out." He picked up his keys. "I'll be home later."

After stewing for a little while, I headed to Zach's. It wasn't fair that I'd made him wait so long for an answer.

CHAPTER 22

*W*hen I was almost to Zach's front door, the sound of his guitar stopped me. He was out on the back porch.

I took the path around the house, ready to surprise him on the patio. That serene space had become our spot.

Voices were drowned out by the music, but then he stopped playing.

"I'm sorry things didn't work out with Haley, but it looks like you've gotten over it." Why was Hank here? Where was his truck?

"What are you talking about?" Zach didn't bother to hide the irritation in his voice.

"Your cat, Zach. He busted you." Hank laughed.

My stomach fell.

"Crap! Waldo, get back here." Zach's voice drew closer.

Positioned like a catcher, I was ready, and when Waldo bolted around the corner, I caught that cat and took back what was mine. "I've been looking for these."

Zach ran into view and stopped. "Hey." He glanced back toward the porch. "Does this mean you're ready to talk?"

Pointing to Waldo, he shook his head. "I had no idea he'd stolen those."

I put Waldo down. "I know. You said you'd put my things in my bag, but of my lacy things, only my bra made it home. And yes, I'm ready, but you have company. I can—"

"He can wait." Zach touched my cheek. "I want to hear what you have to say."

For all the time I'd taken to think about things, the answer I'd planned wouldn't come out of my mouth. My head and my heart didn't agree. And my heart was right.

I'd come prepared to be the dutiful sister, putting family above all else. But I was no longer the little kid who believed all the rules her older brother laid out. If I walked away from Zach now, I'd regret it forever.

Inching forward, I put a hand on his chest and looked up at him. "I can't think of the right words to say. Maybe if you kiss me, it'll help me think."

My feet left the ground as he pulled me against him. "With pleasure."

Kissing Zach, I forgot that my brother was around the corner. Until he wasn't.

"What in the world?" Hank pointed at my hand, where I was clutching what Waldo had stolen. "They're *hers*?" He turned a shade I'd never seen before.

Zach nudged me behind him and turned to face Hank. "It's not what you think."

"You lied to me. You said there was nothing to be concerned about, but the whole time you were . . . you were *wooing* her."

Now was the wrong time to giggle. Preventing that giggle caused my tongue to bleed a little.

"Wooing, yes. But nothing else." Zach reached back and clasped my hand. "You were worried that if I dated Haley, it would ruin everything. And that's not true. It wouldn't."

Only once before had I ever seen Hank so upset.

He puffed up his chest, then blew out a breath slowly. Rage radiated off him. "Haley, may I borrow your car? Mine's at the shop and won't be ready until morning."

While it wasn't the time for tangents, I couldn't help myself. "How did you get here?"

"Zach met me at the garage down the road. Why? That has nothing to do with . . ." He waved his hands between Zach and me. "Can I have the keys or not?"

"Hank, don't do this. Don't leave." I looked at Zach, then at Hank.

"I'm not staying. You can come with me, or you can give me the keys." He stuck out his hand.

Zach tensed, and his gaze cut to me. "Grow up, Hank. This isn't a game of Truth or Dare. She doesn't have to choose." Sighing, he kissed me on the temple. "Go with your brother."

I hugged him and hoped he understood how much his words meant. Then I hooked a thumb over my shoulder. "Okay, Hank. Let's go."

Hank glared at Zach, then followed me to the car. Once he buckled his seat belt, I drove home.

Silence sat between us like a three-hundred-pound bunny. I've never seen one that big, but I imagine it would be scary and unsettling. The silence wasn't scary, but it was unsettling.

When I pulled into the driveway, Hank opened his door. "Thanks for choosing me."

"I didn't." I leaned across and yanked his door closed. *But I didn't want you driving off with my car.*

He blinked, and I backed out of the driveway.

My phone rang over and over as I drove. Hank could leave his apology on my voice mail. How dare he wedge me into a place where I had to choose between love and family. I mentally corrected myself—a chance at love.

Kissing Zach was exhilarating and fun, but it was the comfort of being liked in spite of my quirkiness that made my heart thud when he focused those green eyes on me. Even if this relationship with him was temporary, I'd kick myself if I didn't take this chance.

Years of thought had been dedicated to him.

I parked next to the Explorer.

Zach was playing the guitar again, so I walked around the house and smiled when I noticed the newly started fire in the center of the pit. "Hi."

He tugged a chair closer to him and patted the seat. "Moon Pies are on that little table, and there's an RC Cola in the cooler."

"You knew I was coming back?"

A weary smile curled his lips. "I hoped."

I sat down. "I feel like I'm messing everything up."

"Hank and I will be fine. Once, in college, we dated the same girl." He strummed a soft tune.

"At the same time?"

"Yep. Neither of us knew for the first week. When he found out—I'd never seen him so mad . . . until tonight. He didn't speak to me for a month. And that was awkward because we were roommates."

"This story is only making me feel worse, Zach."

He laughed. "We got past that. We'll figure this out too."

"How did you figure that out? What happened?" I wanted the step-by-step method to make everything better.

"I stopped seeing her, and Hank dated her until she dumped him a month later."

"You were hoping I wouldn't ask about that part, huh?"

"Right." He continued to play.

I leaned back in the chair and closed my eyes. Sitting here

on the patio with Zach was nearly perfect, but it felt bittersweet.

Zach stopped playing.

I opened my eyes in time to see him tucking the guitar back into the case.

"I hate that you're upset." He brushed at my cheek. "Tears make me uncomfortable."

"I didn't even realize I was crying."

"You need a distraction." He tapped his phone screen, and music started playing. "Will you dance with me?"

"I'd love to."

He slipped an arm around me and held me close as we moved to the music. "And here, Harper won't come barging in."

I laughed.

"That's a sound I love to hear."

"You are the most romantic man ever. Has anyone ever told you that?" I leaned my head on his chest as we danced a circle around the firepit.

Laughter rumbled in his chest. "I've been called a lot of things, but never that."

* * *

ZACH DRAGGED chairs out into the yard, then handed me a blanket. "It's clear, so we have a good chance of seeing meteors."

I snuggled under the blanket. "A warm fire, dancing, Moon Pies, and RC Cola—the night has been full of my favorite things."

"You left something important off your list." He leaned over my chair.

"What's that?"

"Not a what. A who." He brushed his lips on mine. "Thanks for coming back."

"I hope we see lots of shooting stars. I have lots of wishes." I spread the blanket so that it covered him also, then rested my head on his shoulder.

He kissed my head. "Me too."

We lay there, snuggled in the dark.

"Did you get tired of me chasing you and finally gave in?" I kept my gaze fixed on the sky.

He pointed. "Look."

I squeezed his arm and silently made my wish as a tiny fiery ball streaked across the sky.

"I hadn't gotten the memo that you were chasing me. I mean, when we were kids, you always smiled at me like I was something special. And you were always cheering for me. I liked that."

"Keep talking." I used the edge of the blanket to wipe away a stray tear.

"Are you crying? I don't want you to cry." He touched my face.

"Another shooting star." I kissed him. "These are happy tears. Keep going."

"But you were always Carrot, Hank's little sister. Until Thanksgiving."

The night came alive with meteors streaking across the sky. The conversation waited until the light display slowed down.

"I should get you home." He stood and helped me up.

I hugged him. "Tonight turned out much better than I thought. And I have my car here." I gathered the blanket.

"I'd like to drive you home. It's two in the morning." He folded the chairs. "I'll pick you up whenever you want to get your car."

"When do I get to hear the rest of the story?"

Zach grinned. "What do you want to know?"

"When we spoke at Christmas, this didn't seem to be an option." I stuck my hands in my pockets.

He shrugged. "That was before you quit talking to me and before I saw you dancing with Harper."

"You were jealous!"

"I thought that was obvious." He unlocked the Explorer. "If Hank gives you a hard time, I can—we can . . . probably—"

"I'll be fine. But if things get really uncomfortable, Nacha said I could move in with her."

"Because that wouldn't make Hank really mad. You date his best friend and move in with his ex. I see that going really well." Zach clasped my hand.

I hadn't quite thought about it that way. "It's option B."

"We can only hope that option A works out."

CHAPTER 23

Saturday morning, I woke up giddy and eager for Eve to get home. I couldn't wait to fill her in on all that had happened since the wedding. Staying in bed meant I didn't have to face Hank, so I enjoyed my happy bubble a little longer.

But when Zach's Explorer pulled in the driveway—I'd become somewhat of an expert at identifying the sound of his engine—I hopped out of bed. Hank opened the front door as I walked down the hall.

"Hank, I don't want to fight." Zach was standing out of my line of sight.

Hank picked that moment to take a swing.

Less than a second later, Zach had Hank pinned to the wall. "I said I didn't want to fight."

"Quit it! Both of you." My worst nightmare was playing out before my eyes.

Zach threw his hands up in surrender and stepped back. "I'm here to take him to pick up his truck. He texted me that it was ready."

Hank stared at me, blinking. "You're here."

"I moved in weeks ago, Hank. Of course I'm here." I hugged Zach. "Are you okay?"

"He didn't get me. I was kind of expecting it." He brushed hairs out of my face. "Please don't be upset."

I whipped around and glared at my brother. "What is wrong with you, Hank? Seriously?"

Zach stepped behind me and snaked an arm around my waist. "Is no one good enough for your sister, or is it just me who doesn't measure up?"

The question broke my heart.

Hank shook his head. "Haley's car isn't here. And the cat had her . . ." He scrubbed his face. "I thought . . ."

"My cat has issues. Good taste, but serious issues. And I drove Haley home because we watched the meteor shower last night." Zach stuck out his hand. "Truce?"

Hank eyed the extended hand but didn't shake it. "I need some time."

"What you need right now is your truck. Let's go." Zach pulled open the door. "When I come back, I'll take you to breakfast, Carrot. If you want."

Breakfast and Zach sounded like the perfect morning. "I'll be ready."

I watched them walk out to the Explorer, hoping they'd both make it back alive. Once they were out of sight, I ran back down the hall.

Somewhere between my shower and putting on shoes the perfect idea popped in my head.

Hank himself had told me the solution, but I was too wrapped up in everything to realize it. There was one person who made Hank a better person, who made him see reason. Clearly it didn't always work because they were divorced, but I needed Nacha.

I texted Zach: *Where are you taking me? I want to invite Hank along.*

He sent the name of the restaurant. *I already asked. He said no.*

My perfect plan would have to wait.

* * *

AFTER A QUIET DRIVE to the restaurant, I slid into a booth.

Zach tapped my arm. "Scooch over. I'll sit next to you."

"Are you worried?"

He draped an arm around me and looked over the menu. "He'll come around. We'll invite him next weekend. And every weekend after until he says yes."

"I want you to know, that if this doesn't work—if we have a falling out—I will still want Hank to be your friend."

"I know." He closed his menu and scanned the room.

Instead of feeling nervous jitters, I felt an ease around Zach. "This is strange."

"Yeah. Usually the waitress comes to the table right away."

I poked him in the side. "That's not what I meant. You and me. In some ways, it feels like we've been dating for months."

"A few good rounds of Truth or Dare, and we'd be up to a year in no time." He smiled as the waitress approached the table.

"Sorry about making you wait. We had a mini disaster in the kitchen, but it's all good now." She flipped open her ordering pad. "What can I get y'all?"

"I'll take the special with extra bacon. And a coffee."

Zach handed over the menus. "I'll take the same. She'll need cream and sugar."

"Coming right up." The waitress hurried away.

"Like that. You know what I want in my coffee."

"I noticed."

"And that means something to me." I waited for him to

say something, but when he didn't, I continued. "Seeing me dance with Harper changed your mind about us?"

"You are seriously chatty before coffee." He tilted his head back. "Let me have a cup or two; then I'll talk about my feelings as long as you want."

This was a side of Zach I hadn't seen.

"You faked it pretty well earlier. I'm sorry you had to duck Hank's punches before you'd even had coffee."

He gave a slow nod.

I really would have to wait until he had coffee.

The waitress arrived with the coveted black gold, and Zach downed half a cup before I'd doctored mine to perfection.

He flashed a smile. "I'm definitely going to need more than one cup, but this is a good start. And like I told you last night, this isn't the first time Hank and I have been at odds."

"I've never seen you fight before."

"You must not have been tagging along then." He played with my curls.

"I hate that I'm the reason."

"It's not the only time you've been the reason for a fight." He leaned back as the waitress set plates on the table. "Thank you so much. This looks great."

"I'll check in with y'all in a bit, hun." She moved on to the next table.

"You can't drop a comment like that and not give me more information." I shook my head as he picked up his fork. "Tell me."

"Eat first." He kissed my temple.

The suspense made me hungry.

True to his word, before I'd consumed my extra bacon and after he'd finished his second cup of coffee, Zach patted my hand. "I'll talk now."

"What do you mean it's not the first time you've argued

with Hank about me?"

"He hated having you tag along. To me, it wasn't a big deal. You laughed at my jokes. But the only time we really fought was when I suggested that you go camping with us."

"I've never been camping with the two of you."

"Because I didn't win that fight."

"You fought about it? As in throwing punches? Why would you do that?" The story made me angry at my brother, but it gave me a different perspective on Zach.

He chewed his lip a second. "I'm trying to figure out how to say this without putting my foot in my mouth."

"Just say it." I looped my arm around his. "I can handle it."

"I didn't have any sisters . . . or brothers for that matter. And I never thought of you as any more than Hank's little sister. I haven't been harboring a secret crush on you for years, but I liked having you around."

"Nothing you just said explains anything about a fight. But I'm flattered that you didn't mind having me around." I made sure my last sentence dripped with sarcasm.

He laughed. "We had a camping trip planned. It was right after I'd gotten dumped in the middle of the cafeteria. You probably heard about that."

"Back when you were in high school?"

"Yep. My sophomore year."

"Is that when the girl poured milk on your tray and announced in front of the whole room that you kissed like a fish?" I'd paid entirely too much attention to Zach's life over the years.

"Clearly, you do remember."

"Want to know what I would've asked her if I'd been there?"

"I do now."

"I'd have asked how she knew what kissing a fish felt like."

Laughing, he kissed the top of my head. "And that's why I

173

like you. Anyway, I thought having you around on the campout would lift my spirits. It totally would have. But Hank did not agree. He thought—it made him mad. We exchanged a couple of punches, and I never again suggested that you come camping with us."

"But then Hank had the grand plan that we should all camp together at Thanksgiving."

"That was all his idea. A good one." Zach poked me in the side. "But I'm sorry you got hurt."

"Any other stories I don't know about?"

"Tons." He bumped his shoulder against mine. "I almost asked you to prom—"

"You had a date to prom. Ugh, I couldn't stand her."

"I meant your prom. We were home for a weekend not long before the big day, and I heard you crying to Eve about missing it." He held his fingers close together. "I was this close to asking you but decided it wouldn't be worth the fallout from your brother."

"What made it worth it now? Jealousy?" I stared at my last piece of bacon, wondering if I had room.

"I didn't like seeing you dance with Harper, but that didn't bother me as much as you not talking to me. But what really changed my mind was actually something you said."

I laid the piece of bacon on his plate and waited for him to continue.

"You said that Adam would do anything for Eve. I thought about that a lot." He nodded when the waitress held up the pot of coffee. "I like seeing you smile, and I really like it when I'm the one that puts it there. Gosh, I haven't talked this much since I don't remember when."

My heart bubbled with emotion. "I'm enjoying it."

"Now, it's my turn for a question."

"Okay." I pushed my cup closer to the edge so she'd refill mine too.

He rested an arm on the back of the bench and played with my hair. "Why haven't you adopted a dog?"

The waitress refilled our cups. "Here's your check, but no hurry. Y'all cuddle here as long as you want."

"Thanks." Zach pushed my mug back toward me.

I opted to take the easy route with my answer. "I've only been living there a few weeks, and it's been busy."

"Haley Sparks, I want the real reason." He lifted one eyebrow. "If this is going to work, you have to be honest with me. I poured out my soul."

I grabbed a napkin, ready if the dam broke. "I can't get another dog at the house. It's silly, but whenever I'm in that backyard, I can only think of Comet." I swallowed and held back the tears. "That's his yard."

"That's not silly." He kissed the top of my head. "Makes perfect sense. One day, you'll live somewhere else, and that yard will need a dog."

"I'm glad I moved back into the house. I might not be saying that at the end of the week, but we'll see."

"Hopefully, Hank comes around quickly. You ready?" He finished the last of his coffee. "I think we should play a game of Cornhole, just you and me."

"What am I playing for?"

"A kiss."

"And if I lose?"

That mischievous smile made his green eyes sparkle. "You give me a kiss."

"That's the exact same thing."

"But you still want to win, don't you?" He slid out of the booth and held out his hand. "Then maybe we can play a game of Truth or Dare."

"I'm not sure if I'm ready for that. I get the feeling there is no dare you won't attempt."

He shrugged. "You won't know until we play."

175

CHAPTER 24

*A*fter two weeks of dating Zach, I wanted him for my happily-ever-after. Things with Hank were still strained—as in, he wasn't speaking to me, but at Zach's, it was easier to pretend everything was fine.

Loaded down with my laptop, camera, and groceries, I kicked on the front door.

Zach pulled it open then finished pulling on a T-shirt. I hadn't lied when I told Lisa the man looked great without a shirt.

"Hiya. Good timing. I just got home. What's this about you making dinner?" He took the grocery bags out of my hands.

"Good. You got my message." I dropped my stuff near the door and followed him into the kitchen. "You are always cooking for me, so I thought I'd return the favor. And I have a surprise."

He pulled me into his arms. "A surprise, huh?"

"I think you'll like it."

Pretending to tickle me, he wiggled his fingers near my sides.

I wriggled and blocked his hands, an involuntary giggle punctuating my moves.

"I don't even have to touch you. The air around you is ticklish." He kissed my forehead. "You're so much fun."

"I do that because I think you're going to tickle me. It's a reflex."

"It's cute and extremely entertaining." He pulled groceries out of the bags. "There are veggies in here. Now I'm curious."

"I'm making meatloaf, but it'll have veggies in it."

"You know I'm only teasing when I give you a hard time, right?"

I nodded and prepped ingredients.

"You don't have to change anything for me."

"I know."

He leaned back against the counter. "And I've been thinking. If you don't like me calling you Carrot, I'll stop."

"Now who's talking about changing?"

"You know what I mean."

I washed my hands, then slid my arms around his waist. "You are the only one allowed to call me Carrot. If Hank starts, I'll whap him."

"You like it when I call you that?"

"I used to feel little and patronized when you called me that. I don't anymore."

"I *never* meant for it to make you feel bad. You were just my favorite carrot top."

"I like *that* word—favorite."

"Good to hear." He patted my hips. "I should let you cook."

"Hungry?"

"Very!" He laughed. "I'm not hard to figure out, am I?"

"That's not what I thought the night of the wedding." I shooed him out of the kitchen. "Now, go."

* * *

"Patio or sofa?" Zach closed the dishwasher. "If you want the patio but are too cold, I'll grab you a sweatshirt."

"Patio and a sweatshirt." I stirred the hot chocolate. "I'll serve this up and meet you out there."

I ladled Mexican hot chocolate into two mugs. Then I wiped the counter to clean up all that I'd dribbled in the process.

He already had his guitar out when I walked onto the patio. "The sweatshirt is in your chair."

Once the hot chocolate was safely on the little table, I pulled his sweatshirt over my head. "Is this how you spent your evenings before I came into the picture?"

"Pretty much. Sometimes I read or played video games. Or Hank and I would shoot hoops. My life isn't all that exciting."

I loved that his life was quiet and settled. "Truth or dare?" The hot chocolate had the perfect zing of cinnamon and the warmth I craved.

He grinned. "Truth."

"I was sure you'd pick dare."

"Just trying to keep you on your toes." He stopped strumming. "Ask away."

"I don't know what to ask you."

He laughed. "I'll ask you one while you think of what you want to ask me."

"Okay. Should I be worried?" I jumped when fur brushed my ankle. "Look who's here."

Waldo hopped up onto my chair and curled up near my feet.

"He likes you." Zach tapped his chin. "How long have you been crushing on me?"

Chocolate went down the wrong pipe, and I coughed.

He squatted beside my chair and patted my back. "I wasn't trying to kill you with my question."

"Funny. But I'm pretty sure it's possible to die of embarrassment." I caught his arm as he moved back toward his chair. "Mostly you surprised me."

"Like you surprised me by putting zucchini and carrots in the meatloaf."

"I've been crushing on you since you and Hank first started hanging out. I didn't do well keeping it a secret, I guess." I shivered and crossed my arms.

Zach scooped me up. "Come on, Waldo. We can cuddle next to her inside." He dropped onto the couch with me still in his arms. "I didn't know."

"The first morning after you kissed me, Hank accused me of being after you since day one. So, maybe, that's why I choked on the question."

"If I'd known, I never would've asked."

"But I was silly then."

His eyebrows shot up in surprise. "Silly? My poor ego."

"When I worked up the nerve to ask you to go with me to my eighth-grade dance—"

"I'd have been a senior then."

I nodded. "Well, I was practicing in front of the mirror—trying out intonation, figuring out when to smile. Hank walked by and dropped a bomb on my plan. He told me as a little sister, I was never allowed to date his best friend. And silly me, I believed him."

Zach started to say something, but I put a finger to his lips.

"I'm happy with the way it worked out. I'm so much more impressed now."

"I look better with my shirt off, huh?" Those dazzling green eyes danced with humor.

I cradled his face. "Your patio is amazing. And the way you smoke a brisket . . . be still my heart."

He tipped me backward and hovered a finger near my stomach.

I reacted exactly as I had before.

"I'm not touching you." He laughed as I wriggled.

"You better be because you are the only thing keeping me from falling on my head."

He pulled me back to his chest. "You never asked me my question."

"I'll save it for later."

"Any change with Hank?"

"Nope. He occasionally breaks his silence and asks me where I hid the remote." I glanced at the time. "I should probably head home. Thank you for letting me come over."

"Do you hide the remote?"

"Yep."

"Before you go, I want to show you something."

"What?" I hadn't expected show and tell.

He clasped my hand and led me out to the back porch. "You can come over here anytime you want. I keep a spare key hidden out here. See that rock in the wall around the firepit?" He kicked at a stone. "Pull on it."

I tugged on the rock, and it slid right out. The inside was hollowed out just enough to make room for a key.

"Use it whenever you want. Only you and Hank know it's there."

"Is this a hint that you want me to sneak in and make you dinner every night?"

He slid his hands down my sides. "I wouldn't complain a bit."

I inched up on my toes and danced my fingers in his hair. "Then maybe I'll do that."

As our lips met, he picked me up. Who knew that all the

practice carrying me at Thanksgiving would come in so handy?

CHAPTER 25

*B*usiness was getting busier, which sometimes meant long hours. But it was rewarding to see our photography sessions booked. Word of mouth was a powerful marketing tool.

Nacha walked into my office. "Busy tonight? I thought maybe we'd grab dinner."

"Sure." Since she never asked me to dinner, I wasn't about to say no. "Let me shut down the computer; then I'll be ready."

"Sounds good." She closed my office door on the way out.

I dialed Zach. "Hi, I wasn't sure if you'd be able to answer."

"It's your lucky day. How's my favorite person?"

Having him talk to me that way never got old.

"Nacha invited me to dinner." I hated to cancel dinner plans with Zach.

"We have dinner together almost every night. Waldo and I will survive an evening without you. Go out with Nacha. I think that's important."

"Thanks. I agree."

"Call me later."

Talking to him was the way I ended every day. We'd been dating almost three weeks, and my lifetime infatuation had evolved into something deep and lasting.

"You know I will." I bit back the *Love you* that threatened to slip out. It was way too soon for that. I shut off the computer and grabbed my purse. "I'm ready."

"I was thinking we'd go to my place and have something delivered."

"Great plan." I hadn't been in the house since Hank moved out. The evening had the possibility of being awkward.

I met her at the house.

She swung open the door and crossed her arms. "I hope you don't mind that we came here. I know it's probably awkward after what's happened with me and Hank." Even the way she said his name made it clear she was in love.

Only they can fix their mess. Zach's words played in my head, and I reminded myself not to interfere. If she asked for my advice, I'd give it. Otherwise, I'd keep my mouth closed.

"This is fine." I dropped my purse and sat on the sofa.

She pulled her phone out of her pocket. "Pizza or Pad Thai?"

"Pad Thai."

She ordered, then sat in the chair next to the couch. "There really isn't anything going on. We haven't done this in a while, and I wondered how things were with Zach . . . and Hank. Did he finally come around?"

I shook my head. "He's hurt and angry. Doesn't speak to me or to Zach."

"It's hard when you have a picture in your head, and it shatters. He'll figure it out."

"I'm not sure he will. And it's crushing me."

"Follow me." She jumped up and walked down the hall.

"This room is yours if you want it. I know it's a lot farther from Zach, but please know that you have other options."

"I'll think about it." Two weeks ago, I was mostly against the idea. Now, I entertained the thought.

"Tell me about Zach."

"You mean I haven't bored you to tears yet? I talk about him all the time."

"What do you love most about him?"

I'd asked her the same question about Hank about two years ago. "We aren't using that word."

She rolled her eyes, then walked back out to the living room. "Maybe you aren't saying it."

"I don't have to pretend. I can be me. I'm not always worried if my smile looks natural or if he'll think I'm stupid. For so long, I felt like everything I did around Zach made me look childish. But now, I get the benefit of knowing him forever and the sense that he appreciates me for who I am, quirks and all."

Nacha had been distant since Hank moved out. While our friendship weathered the strain, it wasn't like when we'd first met. This gave me a taste of what we used to have.

"I'm so glad you figured it out because watching the two of you dance around and then act like the other wasn't dancing was maddening. The way he looked at you that day by the barn made it pretty clear to me he was interested."

"Hank kinda made that difficult. And I feel bad for him because I guess I did steal his friend, but—"

"Don't even think like that. Hank cares about both of you. He'll realize what he's lost." She jumped up to grab the food from the delivery guy.

Maybe I should talk to her about her relationship with Hank. What could it hurt?

The answers pelted my brain—our friendship, the business, her heart. I'd keep my mouth shut on that topic for now.

"Why don't we head to the table to eat?" She carried the food into the kitchen.

"This is nice. We haven't done this in a long time."

She didn't look up. "If you want me to talk to Hank, I'm willing to do that."

I hugged her. "It means so much that you'd even offer to do that. I'll see how tomorrow goes. It might come to that. You know him better than anyone."

She gave a slight nod. "Once upon a time, I did."

"Let's eat. This looks great."

Her shoulders relaxed. "Smells good too. I'm hungry."

I hadn't exactly promised Zach I wouldn't interfere, but even if I wanted to venture down that road, Nacha wasn't ready.

* * *

WHEN I CLIMBED into the car, I shot off a courtesy text to Zach. Letting him know my comings and goings had become habit. *I'm leaving Nacha's.*

I'm still up. That was all the invitation I needed.

Be there soon. I headed to Zach's.

He met me at the front door. "How did it go?"

"It was fun. She and I used to hang out like that before Hank came on the scene. Then she spent most of her time with him. Then she stopped spending time with everyone."

"You didn't try to fix things for them, did you?"

I crossed my heart. "I didn't. It was hard though. She's still in love with Hank. It's obvious in the way she talks about him."

Zach scooped me up and carried me to the sofa. "Promise me you won't play matchmaker."

"Or what?"

"I'm not going to threaten you, Carrot."

I sat up and straddled his lap. "I promise."

His arms circled me. "This is so much better than a phone call."

"I was glad you were still up."

He gazed at me a full minute before pulling me to his lips, and we spent the next few minutes doing what we couldn't do over the phone.

I rested my head on his shoulder. "She offered me her extra bedroom again."

"Are you going to move?"

"I'm thinking about it."

He trailed his fingers up and down my back. "If you decide to do that, I'll help you move."

"You don't think it's a bad idea?"

"I didn't think Hank would pout this long. I'll support whatever you decide to do."

"Thank you."

He lifted me out of his lap. "It's getting late. You have to see straight to take pictures tomorrow."

"True. I should go." I held his hand as I walked to the door.

"Carrot, you know where my key is. Use it whenever you want."

I hadn't shown up unannounced yet. "I'll use it when I need it. With the way things are, this feels more like home than my house."

It was true, but it had nothing to do with the structures.

His goodbye kiss felt like butterflies dancing on my lips. "Night. Text me when you get home."

I kissed his cheek. "I will."

CHAPTER 26

$\mathscr{I}$ walked into the kitchen as Hank closed the refrigerator. "Hi. How was your week?"

He carried his bottle of water out of the kitchen, ignoring my question. The front door closed a minute later, and his truck backed out of the driveway.

Three weeks of putting up with Hank's cold shoulder had taken its toll. I wasn't staying home tonight to endure his drama. In fact, I wasn't going to stay here anymore. Tomorrow, I'd let Nacha know I was going to move in with her.

I picked up the remote, trying to decide where to hide it. I slipped into Hank's room and dropped it into his underwear drawer. He wouldn't blame me for that. Since it was buried under the stuff in the back—that Nacha had given him—he might never find it.

I left the house before he got back so I didn't have to pretend I had no idea where the remote was.

Spending the evening with Zach had become routine, but he was working late. And I made it a point not to bother Eve after work now that she was married . . . at least until the newlywed phase was over. I wasn't even sure how long that phase lasted.

Zach had mentioned the key more than once.

So I went to Zach's even though he wasn't home. I fished his key out of its hidey-hole.

After ordering pizza . . . twice, I stuffed myself and cried until my eyes were red and puffy. Feeling like I'd betrayed my brother, I sobbed. But what hurt worse was that with Zach, I was happy, and Hank wouldn't even acknowledge that.

Why was his happiness more important?

I tugged a blanket up to my chin and curled up on the couch.

Hopefully, Zach would be home soon.

*　*　*

ZACH BRUSHED a finger along my cheek. "Carrot, let's get you into a bed. The way you're curled up, your neck will not be happy in the morning."

I sat up and rubbed my face. "Sorry. I should've told you I was coming. Surprising a guy who carries a gun isn't a great idea."

He sat down and opened his arms.

I crawled into his lap. As much as I wanted things to be right with my brother, I couldn't imagine walking away from Zach. I loved him. Tearing out my heart would be easier.

That was not a pretty word picture.

"You didn't surprise me. If I hadn't noticed the yellow car in the driveway, the pizza boxes on the counter would've been a clue about the redheaded Goldilocks on my couch."

Resting my head on his chest, I wiped my eyes. "I ordered a pizza the way we like it—half all meat, half supreme—but I was so upset, I ate your half too. I didn't even pick off the veggies. So I had to order another one. It's in the fridge."

He wrapped his arms around me. "What has you so upset that you're eating veggies?"

"Hank didn't really do anything different. It's just hard. Doubly so since we're in the house where we grew up. When we silently pass each other in the hall, I can almost see my parents shaking their heads. They'd hate this." I shifted to look Zach in the eye and struggled to restrain my sobs. "And please don't suggest that we stop seeing each other. I mean unless you want to break up with me. If that's the case, then it's okay if you tell me. But please don't let Hank be the reason. And I decided to move out."

In the short time we'd been dating, I'd fallen in love. But I couldn't tell him. Not yet.

"The thought of not dating hadn't even popped into my head." Zach pulled my head back to his chest. "And if you need to cry, that's okay."

When he said that, I sobbed.

He rubbed my back and kissed my head. "I'm sorry. I thought that after three weeks, Hank would've been okay with everything."

"Before, I thought maybe I should have Nacha talk to him. He said himself that she makes him a better person. And last night, she offered."

Zach shook his head. "I don't think that's a good idea. Not at all." He kissed my forehead. "I'll handle it."

"How? You going to let him slug you until he feels better?" I worked to catch my breath.

He gave a quick huff of a laugh. "Let's consider that option B."

"I thought moving in with Nacha was option B."

"Then we'll label it option C."

"What are you going to do?"

"I'll think of something."

* * *

THE NEXT AFTERNOON, I'd almost forgotten Zach's assurance that he'd handle things. But needing a distraction, I'd arranged to go shopping with Nacha after work. While we were out, I'd let her know about my decision to move in.

"I'm sorry we had to go out of our way, Nacha. I'm the worst about spilling stuff on myself." I fished my keys out as she drove through Stadtburg.

She stopped for a light, one of three in town. "You stayed at Zach's last night?"

"In the guest room. I'm hoping Hank isn't home because I really don't want a lecture." I hadn't brought up moving into her extra bedroom.

"You going over there again tonight?" She asked more questions than usual.

I shifted in my seat. "Maybe. I don't know. Zach knows we're going shopping, so he's not expecting me until later."

She turned onto my street, and I gasped.

"That's Zach's truck. He must've come over here after work. I didn't think this was what he meant by 'I'll handle it.' Please don't let them be fighting."

She slammed the car into park as soon as she turned into the driveway. "I'm coming in with you."

The front door was unlocked, and we slipped inside unnoticed.

They weren't in the living room.

A chair scraped across the floor in the kitchen, and Zach hollered. "It became my business when she started sobbing on my couch at two in the morning. You want to act like the last twenty years didn't happen and we were never friends? Fine! But don't do this to her. Don't!"

"You don't understand at all." Hank shouted even louder.

I stepped forward, but Nacha caught my arm.

"Let them finish." She inhaled, clearly as bothered as I was.

"You're right, Hank. I don't understand. I'm your best friend. But I need you to understand that I *love* your sister."

"You *think* you love her. It won't last."

"You're wrong. With her, I don't have to filter every word out of my mouth, concerned I might say something that she'll twist into an insult. I don't get home after dealing with an unsettling crime scene and worry that she'll take my bad mood personally. I can be myself with her. She's funny and quirky and tailored for me. It's like I was always meant to love her. And I think she loves me too." He paused. Was he choked up?

I was.

Nacha hugged me.

"I spent years thinking it was a fun game trying to make Carrot laugh when she'd tag along. But I didn't realize until a few months ago—it's more than a game. I like making her laugh. I love being responsible for the smile on her face. And, Hank, I know you understand. I saw the way you were with Nacha—"

"Leave her out of this," Hank snapped.

Nacha bolted toward the kitchen. So much for letting them finish. "Zach, please give us a minute."

"What are you . . ." Hank didn't finish his question.

Zach walked into the living room and gave me a weak smile. "You heard?"

I nodded. Talking wasn't possible at that moment.

He pulled me into his arms.

We both braced for the conversation in the kitchen.

"Hank, what is wrong with you? Are you determined to destroy everyone's happily-ever-after? It wasn't enough that you broke my heart? Now you want to do the same thing to Zach and Haley? Is that it?"

"No." He sounded like a chastised child.

My grand plan wasn't so grand after all. Nothing about what she said was soothing.

"That's what you're doing. Anyone can see that they care about each other. He makes her happy. All day, it's 'Zach this and Zach that.' Do you understand what I'm saying?"

Hank didn't say anything, but maybe he nodded. I couldn't see, and it seemed rude to peek around the corner.

"If you don't grow up, Haley's moving in with me. What do you think of that?"

"I don't want anyone else to leave me." Hank's words were barely audible.

I buried my face in Zach's chest.

"Then you should quit pushing people away." Nacha stopped in the doorway and looked back over her shoulder. "And I wasn't the one who left." Wiping her tears, she walked past us and out the front door.

Zach kissed the top of my head. "We should probably go."

Lacing my fingers with his, I followed him to the door.

"Zach, Haley, wait." Hank shoved his hands in his pockets. "Did she leave?"

"She's outside." I stepped toward him. "We only came by so I could change my shirt. I didn't know you'd both be here. I never meant for her . . ."

He shrugged. "Don't worry about it. I deserved it." He rubbed the toe of his shoe on a spot where soda had spilled on the carpet. "Would you really move out?"

"Yes, I quit unpacking boxes weeks ago, and I started packing last night. You don't even speak to me." I moved back toward Zach. "Is it really so awful for me to be dating Zach?"

Hank shook his head. "It's just different. I don't want to feel like the tagalong."

That was something I knew well. "It's not all that bad."

He laughed. "Funny."

"We should go camping this weekend." Zach had to be talking to Hank because I knew he wasn't inviting me.

"Yeah." Hank looked up. "I'm sorry I've been so . . ."

"So what?" I pinched my lips to keep from laughing.

"Really, Haley?" He scratched his head. "I'll say it just to make you happy. I've been stupid and horrible to both of you. I really hope it's not too late for y'all to forgive me." He stared out at Nacha's car. "I wasn't trying to destroy anyone's happily-ever-after."

I seriously needed to find a way to get those two into a room together for a civil conversation. Even during the uncivil one, they'd communicated more than they had in months. But I'd promised Zach I wouldn't play matchmaker. And I intended to keep that promise.

CHAPTER 27

Shopping didn't happen. After the hubbub, I couldn't even remember what I wanted to buy. Nacha barely waited for me to say goodbye before backing out of the driveway.

It hurt to see her upset.

"Hank, I'll see what reservation we can get for tomorrow night, and I'll text you. If you want to come over to the house with us now . . ." Zach let the invitation dangle. Of all times for him to try and be nice.

I silently hoped Hank didn't want to go to Zach's right now.

"Text me. After what Haley overheard—I'm guessing you hadn't told her yet—y'all have stuff to talk about." Hank grinned. "And I'd rather not be in the middle of that one. Awkward."

"So, we're okay?" I really needed the pretty package with the nice little bow.

Hank hugged me. "We're good. Please don't move out."

"I can't promise that I won't move out at some point." Choosing my words carefully, I tried not to make it weird.

Hank rolled his eyes. "I know that. I mean now . . . because of me."

"I won't." I turned to Zach. "I forgot to change my shirt."

"You look beautiful the way you are. Let's go." He tugged me toward the truck.

I wrenched my hand free. "I have a huge red splotch on it."

"Please, can we go to the house? I will let you borrow one of mine." He opened the passenger-side door.

"You're all dressed up today." I ran a finger down the buttons on his dress shirt, then straightened his tie. "Can I have this one?"

"Just don't spill anything on it. I need it for when I go to court." He loosened his tie, then reached for the top button.

Laughing, I swatted his hands. "I was joking."

"I know." He kissed me, then ran around to his side of the truck.

I latched my seatbelt. "I was really surprised—"

"Not yet."

"You don't even know what I was going to say." I grabbed his hand. "But I'll be nice."

He smiled and squeezed my hand.

Five minutes later, we were in his driveway. "Wait here a second." He ran into the house.

Three seconds later, he opened my door. "Okay. Everything is ready."

"Ready for what?"

"What I said earlier—I wanted to tell you face-to-face. I didn't mean for you to hear me shouting it at your brother." He pushed open the front door. "I was going to tell you tonight."

A vase filled with peonies sat in the living room.

"They're beautiful."

"I didn't know your favorite." He tugged me into the kitchen. "So I got a few different kinds."

Zinnias were arranged in a pale blue crock.

"There are roses in the dining room and sunflowers on the back patio." He opened the fridge. "I even had them make up a bouquet of carrots."

"I'm completely overwhelmed . . . in a good way. A seriously good way."

"I know it's only been a few weeks. But I don't need to wait to know that I love you."

"I love you too."

"I know you do." He lifted me onto the counter and cradled my face in his hands. "Now I know what it means when you smile at me like I'm something special. I didn't know that before." Softly and gently, he brushed his lips against mine. "I was about to switch to option C when Nacha ran in."

"That's how much you love me."

"Watching you cry is heart-wrenching." He kissed my hand and set me on the floor. "I'd do *anything* for you."

"I was so surprised to see your truck at the house. When I walked in and heard you—" I swallowed back the lump in my throat. "I never thought I'd be so happy that I walked through poison oak, twisted my ankle, and fell in cactus."

"Me too." He carried me into the living room. "Let me go change; then I'll make us dinner."

"Zach, this is perfect." I didn't let go of his arm. "And I don't really have a favorite flower. You can surprise me with whatever."

He kissed me. "I'll only be two minutes."

"While you change, I'm going to go gather up the other flowers." I sniffed the peonies. "No one has ever given me flowers before."

"It won't be the last time." He blew me a kiss.

* * *

STILL WEARING my shirt with the big stain on it, I leaned back in the lounge chair. The day had ended so much better than it had begun. "I was shocked when Nacha went off on Hank and even more shocked that what she said changed his mind."

"I was glad it ended well. That could've blown up." Zach turned on music and opened his arms. "Care to dance?"

I stepped up close. "Always. Though I was very befuddled, I really enjoyed dancing with you at the wedding."

"If I'd have known dancing with you would make me feel all fluttery, I'd have asked you to prom." He winked.

"You love teasing me, don't you?"

"I love lots of things about you." He twirled me.

I snuggled close as a slow song came on. "I hope you and Hank smooth things out when you go camping. I know he seems okay with it, but I want everything back to normal."

"We will. We'll fish, exchange five, maybe ten words, and settle into a new normal."

"I'm really happy about that." I hated being ignored by my brother, but tearing apart their friendship hurt even worse.

Zach dipped me, then pulled me back to his chest. "I should never have done that to you at Christmas. I'm sorry. My actions said one thing, and my words said another."

"I convinced myself that was your way of trying to be friends."

"You know how many handmade gifts I made?"

The answer was obvious as soon as he asked the question. "One?"

Holding me close, he whispered in my ear. "I planted a cactus for you. A tiny little cactus with spines so teeny, they are hard to see when they get stuck in a finger. Ask me how I know."

"So, I guess maybe you are a bit reckless."

"Only when it comes to you."

I pressed a kiss to his neck. "I love you, Zach."

He danced us to a chair, then pulled me into his lap. Tangling his fingers in my hair, he pulled me close to his lips. "You need to change your ringtone."

"Why are we talking about ringtones? Kiss me."

"Because you don't bring me down." Our lips danced, making our first kiss seem like a playground peck.

I loved this patio almost as much as I loved Zach.

CHAPTER 28

Zach's patio was the favorite gathering spot for our friends during summer. At least once a month, we held a backyard barbecue. He didn't always smoke a brisket, but it was always fun.

And after everyone else had left, Zach and I danced on the patio or gazed at the stars. It was a nearly perfect summer.

My birthday celebration was the last big summer shindig.

Staring up at the dark clouds, I leaned back against Zach. "I don't want it to rain today."

"We need the rain." He dropped kisses on my neck. "And it won't mess up anything—except maybe Cornhole."

"Hank would just beat me anyway."

"And nobody wants to get beat at Cornhole on their birthday. We'll still have brisket, and I'm sure our friends would love to play a round of Truth or Dare." He chuckled. "Did you invite Nacha?"

"Yep, but I'm not playing matchmaker. I won't dare Hank to kiss her or anything like that." I spun around and looped my arms around his neck. "I promise."

"When are people showing up?" After asking the question, he pressed his lips to mine, which made it impossible to answer.

When he broke away, I inched up on my toes, wanting another kiss. "Anytime now. And, um." I inhaled the wonderful smell of smoke on his shirt. "I might need this one too."

"How many of my shirts do you have?"

"No more than five . . . or six."

"I'm going to run out. What will I wear then?"

I tugged at the hem of his shirt. "I'm not seeing a problem."

He laughed. "I'll pull the brisket off and let it sit. It should be ready to slice when people get here."

"And I'll get the veggie tray ready." I waited for his smart retort.

He rolled his eyes. "French fries do not count as a veggie tray."

"Potatoes are a root vegetable just like carrots." My completely valid point would silence him. I hoped.

He grinned, and that twinkle danced in his eyes. "Potatoes aren't a root vegetable. They're a tuber. Still doesn't count as a veggie tray."

The difference between a root and a tuber seemed like a technicality. And what kind of person knew that without looking it up?

Zach was outside before I could think of anything snarky to say.

I slid the tray of fries into the oven, then ran to answer the door.

Hank walked in, and, in a strangely unusual move for him, he greeted me with a hug. Long and tight. "I'm looking forward to today. I can smell that brisket from here. But it looks like a game of Cornhole isn't going to happen."

"We'll have fun anyway. And I wanted you to know that I invited Nacha. I hope you don't mind. She doesn't do much besides work."

His shoulders tensed, and he clenched his jaw a second. "That's fine. I don't mind." He pointed outside. "Zach on the patio?"

"Yep."

"I had no idea she didn't get out much." His voice was almost a whisper.

I patted his arm. "Please don't say anything."

"Of course not." He ran to let Zach in when he carried the brisket toward the door.

I still hadn't figured out a plan to get Nacha and Hank talking. Rather, I hadn't found someone who would concoct a plan to get them talking. But Zach had suggested inviting Nacha today, so I did. Hopefully, she'd come.

Slowly, people arrived.

When Zach ran toward the door after a knock, I leaned around the corner to see who it was. His friends from work were already here. Nacha had come. And Adam and Eve were on the back porch filling a second cooler with drinks.

Who else had Zach invited?

Harper walked in and shook Zach's hand. "Thanks for inviting me."

"Glad you could make it. Food's in the dining room. Drinks are on the patio. Make yourself at home." Zach introduced Harper to a few of the other guests, then walked into the kitchen. "Why are you still in here, Carrot?"

"Making a fresh pitcher of tea." I glanced around to be sure we were alone. "You invited Harper?"

"I told Adam to invite him. You said he was a nice—wait, I think you said he was *a sweet guy*." Zach clapped a hand to his heart.

"You can't seriously be jealous."

He brushed his lips on my ear. "Not in the least. Let's get some food."

"I'll be there in two minutes. But you can go eat."

Eve walked in, grinning. "What time is the second brisket going to be ready?"

Zach paled. "Is it all gone?"

"No, but someone has to give you a hard time." She laughed. "Now go so I can talk to Haley."

He shook his head as he walked into the dining room.

"Soooo? It looks like things are going well. I'm a little surprised y'all invited Harper. Zach didn't look too happy with him at the wedding."

"Zach invited Harper. And things are going really well. It's so hard to believe how much has changed. A little over a year ago, I was peeking through my peephole, watching Zach get dumped."

"Like I said, I have a good feeling about this year."

"I like the way things are. I don't expect things to change quickly. Hank is happy, but I don't want to rock the boat."

"I thought you were past that." Eve's brow knitted. "Would you . . ." She crossed her arms and glanced into the dining room. "Because of Hank?"

Because we were best friends, I understood the words she hadn't said.

"If Zach asked me anything specific—you know what I mean—I'd say yes in a heartbeat. But Zach is being considerate of his friend, and I understand that. Hopefully, Zach knows I'd say yes." Momentary horror made my stomach hurt. "Gosh, I hope he knows. If he asks you, you'll tell him that, won't you?" I straightened the sunflowers on the counter.

"If he asks me, I'll tell him." She fingered the petals. "Those are gorgeous."

"Zach gave them to me this morning. You should've seen

the flowers he gave me last weekend before he and Hank left to go camping."

"When are you going camping with them?" Eve nudged me.

"Never."

"Well, *your* boyfriend has been telling *my* husband how fun camping is. Adam is all excited about the four of us going camping together."

"What?"

Eve poked me in the chest. "And if I have to go camping, you are coming too."

"All right." I put my hands up. "I will, but only if Zach asks. He said he'd *never* go camping with me."

"That was before."

"Yeah, but he ended up with a poison oak rash because of me."

She shrugged. "We'll see, but now you know."

"I've been warned." With my brain a jumble of thoughts about camping and marriage proposals, I followed her into the living room.

Zach tapped the seat next to him. "I fixed you a plate. Brisket, extra veggies, and ranch dressing."

"Exactly what I wanted. Thanks." I popped a bite of brisket in my mouth. "Mmm. This is the best one yet."

Zach beamed. "Happy Birthday."

* * *

ZACH CARRIED the cake into the living room as everyone sang "Happy Birthday." I hadn't been the center of attention in a long time, and I remembered why. I wanted the song to be over.

He dropped to a knee and held out the cake.

"A cactus? Really?" I could feel heat flooding my cheeks.

"With thirty spines all aglow. Blow out the candles and make a wish." He winked.

I made the same wish I'd made when we saw the first shooting star months ago. I was pretty much head over heels then . . . and even more so now. I huffed and blew until all thirty candles were out. Half expecting them to relight, I inhaled again.

Eve ran over and took the cake. "I'll hold this."

"Carrot." Zach hadn't moved. But in his hand was a tiny box with the lid flipped open.

I slapped a hand over my mouth.

"Haley Sparks, we've known each other twenty years. And I'd love to spend the next several decades loving you. Will you marry me?"

"Yes. But are you sure?" The moment seemed too good to be true.

He laughed and pulled me in for a kiss. "I'm sure. I want to go stargazing, dancing, and camping with you until we can barely make it into our rocking chairs. Then I want to sit next to you and do whatever possible to make you smile."

Our friends cheered.

"I'm so happy, but I didn't expect this." I buried my face in the curve of his neck. "You completely surprised me."

Zach kissed my cheek. "I know. That was part of the fun."

"Haley, I want"—Hank cleared his throat—"I want you to know that I'm happy for you. When Zach asked me for your hand, I was excited because you deserve someone like him. And Mom and Dad would be really happy today." He lifted his cup. "To Zach and Haley and a happily-ever-after twenty years in the making."

All our friends raised their cups. "Hear, hear."

After another quick kiss, Zach stood, giving our friends room to swarm.

Eve wiped tears before hugging me. "It was so hard in the

kitchen not to spoil the surprise. And then you gave me the momentary panic." After a long, tight hug, she stepped back. "We'll talk more later. We have a wedding to plan!"

"Whoa, speaking of carrots. This guy went all out." Harper tapped the ring, then hugged me. "Congratulations. It looks like you solved that five-thousand-piece puzzle."

I giggled. "We did."

He squeezed my hand. "I'm glad you didn't throw out the pieces."

"Me too."

For the next hour, I didn't have even a minute alone with Zach. So when Hank—the very last one to leave—walked out the door, I tugged Zach to the couch.

"Thank you. Tonight was so much fun and completely amazing. I don't know how you pulled off this surprise." I sat beside him and draped my legs across his lap. "That's why you wanted me to invite Nacha."

He nodded. "And for good measure, I wanted Harper here to see you say yes . . . to me."

I shifted into his lap. "As if anyone could doubt how I feel about you. But just in case you need to hear it again—Yes. I'm still not sure about the camping part though."

"We'll have fun."

"You said you'd *never* go camping with me." I cocked my head, waiting for his answer.

He tugged at the end of a curl. "And you said you'd *never* date me."

"I can't believe Eve told you that!"

"You know what else she told me?"

I braced for complete embarrassment. "What?"

He tipped me backward and hovered his lips over mine. "Never say never."

EPILOGUE

HANK

ZACH & HALEY'S REHEARSAL DINNER

*I*t had been months since I'd seen Nacha. To say she looked good was an understatement. I'd always love her. And being apart from her was tearing me apart. She hated me, and I still didn't understand why. Asking hadn't gotten me any answers.

Maybe that would change this weekend.

The rehearsal dinner would be starting soon, and I needed to take a seat. But taking a few extra minutes to admire her before joining her at the table seemed like a smart idea. It gave me time to gawk and to compose myself. This weekend was all about my sister and her wedding. And my best friend, but Zach knew he was lucky to be marrying Haley.

After I'd been a bit of a jerk—more like a royal jerk—when Haley and Zach started dating, this weekend needed to be perfect for them, and causing a scene with Nacha would be less than perfect. I'd be on my best behavior. I had an entire weekend at the resort to be with her. If I knew what to do to win her back, I'd give up everything and do it.

I sucked in a deep breath and wove through the tables for two. Was it Aunt Joji or Haley who planned it this way? I wanted to hug whoever had made that decision. Nacha sat alone at a table across the room, and I had no doubt that the name card at the empty spot beside her had my name on it.

She slipped a chunk of dark chocolate out of her purse and popped it into her mouth. Her anxiety must be running high. Once upon a time, she'd run to me instead of chocolate when stress got to her. This time, I was the stress.

My sister Haley greeted people and was obviously making her way toward Nacha, and so I hung back, giving them a chance to talk.

Haley's red curls were all done up fancy, and her smile was as bright as always. When she got to Nacha's table, she danced a jig, her arms spread wide. "Isn't this fabulous? My Aunt Joji booked this for us as a wedding present. I think she was still trekking through Europe or climbing a mountain when you got married. Have you met her?"

To my knowledge, Nacha hadn't had the pleasure of meeting my Aunt Joji. She was eccentric and full of life. It was nice to have her home.

Nacha shook her head. "I haven't."

"I can't wait for you two to meet." Haley leaned in closer to whisper, but I was too far away to hear.

Then they hugged.

"I wouldn't have missed it." Nacha ran her hands down her hips, and I tracked the movement.

When I married Nacha, I thought for sure we'd found our happily ever after. Now my heart ached to be around her.

Haley inhaled and puffed the air out slowly. "I'm nervous. Not about getting married tomorrow. It's all the people watching me. That's what makes me nervous."

"That's why we hide behind the camera." Nacha nodded toward the photographer.

My sister laughed. "Right? But, seriously, thanks for not complaining about coming as a guest. I know it isn't easy."

"I'll be fine." Nacha pointed at Zach across the room. "Someone is looking for you."

Haley squeezed her arm. "I'll find you later, okay?"

Zach met her halfway across the room. He tugged at the end of a curl, then whispered in her ear. How did they make it twenty years before realizing they were like magic together? Probably because of me.

Nacha picked up her phone and snapped a few pictures. Always the photographer. She wouldn't want to miss capturing the look on Zach's face. He clearly loved my sister.

Other guests made their way to tables, and I continued toward Nacha. Seated near the wall, she looked like she was trying to blend in. But in that smoking hot yellow dress, she stood out. I'd bought it for her on our honeymoon, and I loved that she was wearing it tonight.

Focused on her phone, she tensed as I approached the table and didn't look up. There seemed to be a wall of ice around her.

"Nacha." I dropped into the other chair at the table. "Hi."

After a deep breath, she plastered on a smile. "Hello. You look good, Hank."

Her gaze slid down, then snapped back up. At least she still found me attractive.

I leaned on the table and folded my arms. "Thanks."

Even though I'd already admired from across the room, I let my gaze sweep over her again. "You look—you always look good. Today, you look especially good."

She pulled her shoulders back and clasped her hands together. "Thank you."

"It's still hard to believe Haley is marrying my best

friend." I fiddled with the name card, regretting how hard I'd made it for them. "They look happy, don't they?"

"Very happy." She knotted her fingers even tighter, then glanced at my hand on the name card.

With me, nerves and repetition went hand in hand. She knew that. But I stopped because the tapping was like someone drilling into her head. I had to control my nerves some other way.

Laughter echoed through the room as Zach picked up Haley. Her shoe went flying, which only made the guests laugh harder.

He knew exactly how to distract her and make her forget about the crowd watching.

And the way he looked at her made my heart ache for what I'd lost. I snuck a side glance at Nacha. "That used to be us." I pushed my chair back and stood. "I'm going to find something to drink. Want anything?"

It was hard being close to her and feeling so removed. This weekend would be long. But I hoped it would be pivotal. If nothing else, maybe I could figure out what went wrong and try to fix it.

"Yes. Preferably something they won't serve to people under twenty-one." She continued watching Haley and Zach.

"My thoughts exactly." I wandered toward the bar at the back of the room, knowing Nacha would want something strong and sweet.

As I stood at the bar, I flexed because I could feel her watching me. After barely eating for the first few months after she filed for divorce, I changed directions and started working out more. What else was I supposed to do with my free time?

I ordered our drinks and strolled back to the table, and all the while, she pretended not to watch me.

I set a glass in front of me. "Vanilla, Coke, and Vodka."

"Perfect."

She was perfect. In every way, and I wanted to tell her that. But afraid to rock the boat, I dropped back into my chair and sipped my drink.

Aunt Joji with her wild copper curls walked up to our table. "Hank Sparks, introduce me to your bride. I was so sorry to miss the wedding. Has it really been eighteen months since then?"

What was my aunt doing? She knew Nacha and I divorced. Her gushing and acting like everything was still hunky dory wouldn't help the weekend go smoothly. But this wasn't the place to set the record straight.

"Aunt Joji, hi. This is Nacha."

Nacha shot me a look and the questions that flashed in her dark eyes were clear. But I wasn't going to air our dirty laundry at the rehearsal dinner.

She flashed a smile, genuine but nervous. "I've heard so much about you."

Aunt Joji wrapped Nacha in a hug, and the sleeve of Aunt Joji's flowy muumuu landed in my drink. "I like you. People with interesting names should stick together. And I'm so sorry about the confusion with your room."

My aunt had that tone. And worry knotted in my stomach.

Nacha waved her hand. "It's fine. I used Haley's room to get ready."

Aunt Joji tapped her sides, then stuck a hand in her pocket. "Here they are." She handed me a keycard and then to my horror, handed one to Nacha without distinguishing between them. "They bumped y'all up to one of the nicer suites. And I added an extra night. Enjoy!" Waving, she floated through the room.

Nacha grabbed the table, her knuckles turning white. "She thinks we're still . . . married."

My aunt knew. We hadn't talked about it since she'd been back, but she knew. "I haven't seen her in ages. And with everyone so happy about the wedding, I didn't bring it up." Saying more would start a fight, and I didn't want Nacha mad at Aunt Joji.

She finished off her drink, then turned those dark eyes on me. "Fix it. I don't care what you have to do. Fix it."

"I will." I nodded and sprang up out of my chair as the waiter started serving dinner. Eating would have to wait. "I'll do it right now."

I glanced at my sister before slipping out of the room. Sitting at the front, Zach and Haley captivated the room. The way the two of them looked at each other would make even the most hard-hearted believe that fairy tales could come true. But thoughts like that would only make the weekend harder.

At the front desk, I rang the little bell and waited.

A clerk slipped out of the back. "How can I help you?"

"I need a room for tonight. Whatever you have."

His face scrunched up like he'd just nibbled on a lemon. "We don't have any vacancies. Totally full. Because of the wedding."

I leaned forward, needing him to understand how important it was. "Please. I need a room. I don't care if it has a twin bed or if I have to sleep on the floor. Please."

Lemon face returned. "Nothing. Sorry. There is a somewhat low-budget motel about forty miles from here. That's the nearest place. Would you like me to find their number for you?"

"Nothing? Are you sure?"

"Completely booked. Someone booked up the last few just a bit ago." This time he smiled, and it felt like salt in the wound.

How was I going to tell Nacha that she and I would be sharing a suite for the weekend?

I dropped back into my chair and downed my drink, the one that had been tainted with the sleeve. I should have grabbed a second drink before sharing good news. "They're full. With wedding guests."

"What about the room I was supposed to have?" She rubbed her temples.

"Believe me, I asked. Begged even. Nothing is available. Someone booked the last few rooms. Be thankful we have a suite."

It was clear that only one of us was thankful that we'd be sharing a suite for the weekend. And it wasn't Nacha.

* * *

THANK you for reading *One Guy I'd Never Date*! I hope you enjoyed Haley and Zach's story. Find out what happens with Hank and Nacha in *Two Words I'd Never Say Again*. You'll see a different side of Hank, one that you might fall in love with.

Keep reading for a BONUS EPILOGUE!

BONUS EPILOGUE

ZACH

*H*aley's porcelain leg hung over the side of the hammock. Her toes brushed the top of the grass as the nylon fabric swung back and forth. Holding the phone to her ear with one hand, she waved her other hand as she chatted away. "Aunt Joji, a family vacation would be so much fun."

So much about Haley was animated and fun. I was a lucky man.

That wasn't the first mention of a family reunion-type vacation. I'd have to warn Hank. If Joji planned it, she'd conveniently forget that Hank and Nacha were no longer happily married. Poor Hank still wouldn't talk about the wedding weekend at the resort.

I opened the barbecue pit and shifted the coals. Another half hour and we'd be feasting.

A car door closed out front, and I slipped inside and closed the back door. Hopefully, Aunt Joji would keep Haley talking for a bit longer.

I pulled open the door before the guy had a chance to knock.

He smiled. "Zach Gallagher?"

"That's me." I shook his hand, my gaze fixed on the puppy attached to the leash in his other hand. "Thank you so much for bringing him over."

"A surprise, huh?"

"Yeah, for my wife." I dropped to my knees and scratched the pup behind the ears. "She's going to love you. Waldo won't, but don't get your feelings hurt."

"Looks like you've already filled out everything. So, he's all yours." He handed me a folder.

I grabbed the end of the leash. "The card that they had on his pen, is that in here?" Riffling through the papers, I found it. "Yes. I see it."

"Enjoy." The man gave the dog a pat on the head before walking back to the car.

I dropped down onto the front step. "The card says your name is Comet."

The puppy's tail wagged at the mention of his name.

"I'm hoping you won't mind if we call you CJ."

That tail continued swinging from side to side.

"You ready to meet Haley? I think you'll love her. I do." I pushed open the front door. "I have a whole bunch of stuff for you stashed in the garage. But we'll pull that out later."

I pulled the card out of the folder and dropped the rest of the paperwork on the sofa. As we walked out the back door, Haley wrapped up her conversation.

"Love you too. Bye." She swung her other leg over the side, and my breath caught. She only wore those little shorts at home when no one else was around. I wanted to believe it was because she knew I loved them. Correction. I loved the way she looked in them.

Looking at her phone as she walked toward the porch, she hadn't noticed me or my little friend.

I unhooked his leash. "Go say hi."

The smartest dog I'd ever met jogged toward my favorite girl.

She froze when he sat down near her feet. Her phone hit the ground as she dropped to her knees. "Hello there." She let him lick her face before finally looking up. "Please don't say we're pet-sitting for one of your friends."

"He's yours."

She jumped up and patted her leg as she ran to me. I opened my arms, and she flung her arms around my neck. "Thank you. This yard needs a dog."

"It was a completely impulsive move. I'm not even sure what we'll do with him when we go camping next weekend."

"He'll come with us. He can sleep in our tent."

That did not fit with my plan for camping, but I'd figure something out.

CJ barked when Haley kissed me. If he kept that up, he'd drive my neighbors crazy.

She knelt down again and hugged the dog. "What's his name?"

I held out the card. "I think we should call him CJ."

"Oh, Zach." She slapped a hand over her mouth, and tears pooled in her eyes. "No wonder you adopted him."

"And see that note down there. He loves carrots . . . just like me."

With one arm around the dog, she held out her other arm. I knelt beside her and joined the family huddle.

"I think CJ is perfect for little Comet Junior." She could even read my mind. "Remember when I said you were the most romantic man ever?"

I nodded. I'd never forget that night.

"I wasn't wrong." She kissed me again, and CJ started barking.

The neighbors were going to hate us if the dog barked every time we kissed.

She pulled back, and CJ quieted. "I'm not sure if he's excited about me kissing you or jealous."

"If he's jealous, we're going to have a problem."

Waldo skirted the edge of the porch, looking none too happy.

"Speaking of jealous." She giggled and snuggled CJ.

"Me? Never!" I winked.

She wrapped her arms around my waist. "I love you, Zach."

"And I'm glad." I picked her up and pressed my lips to hers.

CJ went nuts.

A NOTE TO READERS

Thank you for reading! This was such a fun story to write. And I'd love to have Zach's porch.

If you loved the story, would you consider leaving a review at your favorite retailer or on Goodreads or Bookbub?

I apologize if the book makes you crave brisket. My husband smoked one while I was writing the book, and I may or may not have sniffed his shirt.

Two Words I'd Never Say Again, Nacha's story, is next in the series.

My other romantic comedy series is set on a ranch right near Stadtburg. Characters from this series show up in that one. If you haven't read *Wrangled by Lilith*, grab a copy today!

Be sure to check out my website at www.PhreyPress.com for information about upcoming releases and to see my other books.

ALSO BY REMI CARRINGTON

Never Say Never

Three Things I'd Never Do

One Guy I'd Never Date

Two Words I'd Never Say Again

One Choice I'd Never Make

Three Rules I'd Never Break

Two Risks I'd Never Take Again

One Whopper of a Love Story

Christmas Love

Christmas Sparkle

Christmas Surprise

Stargazer Springs Ranch

Fall in love with cowboys and spunky women.

Cowboys of Stargazer Springs

The ranch hands are falling in love.

Bluebonnets & Billionaires series

Lots of money & even more swoon.

* * *

Pamela Humphrey, who writes as Remi Carrington, also releases
books under her own name. Visit PhreyPress.com for more
information about her books.

ABOUT THE AUTHOR

Remi Carrington is a figment of Pamela Humphrey's imagination. She loves romance & chocolate, enjoys disappearing into a delicious book, and considers people-watching a sport. She was born in the pages of the novel *Just You* and then grew into an alter ego.

She writes sweet romance set in Texas. Her books are part of the Phrey Press imprint.

facebook.com/remiromance
instagram.com/phreypress

Printed in Great Britain
by Amazon